WHERE'S WALLY?

THE TOTALLY ESSENTIAL
TRAVEL COLLECTION

MARTIN HANDFORD

WALKER BOOKS
AND SUBSIDIARIES
LONDON · BOSTON · SYDNEY · AUCKLAND

HI WALLY-WATCHERS!

ARE YOU READY TO JOIN ME ON MY SEVEN
FANTASTIC ADVENTURES?

> WHERE'S WALLY?
> WHERE'S WALLY NOW?
> WHERE'S WALLY? THE FANTASTIC JOURNEY
> WHERE'S WALLY? IN HOLLYWOOD
> WHERE'S WALLY? THE WONDER BOOK
> WHERE'S WALLY? THE GREAT PICTURE HUNT
> WHERE'S WALLY? THE INCREDIBLE PAPER CHASE

CAN YOU FIND THE FIVE INTREPID TRAVELLERS
AND THEIR PRECIOUS ITEMS IN EVERY SCENE?

ODLAW   WIZARD WHITEBEARD   WENDA   WOOF   WALLY

 WALLY'S KEY   WOOF'S BONE   WENDA'S CAMERA

 WIZARD WHITEBEARD'S SCROLL   ODLAW'S BINOCULARS

WAIT, THERE'S MORE! AT THE BEGINNING AND
END OF EACH ADVENTURE, FIND A FOLD-OUT
CHECKLIST WITH HUNDREDS MORE THINGS
TO LOOK FOR.

WOW! WHAT A SEARCH!

BON VOYAGE!   *Wally*

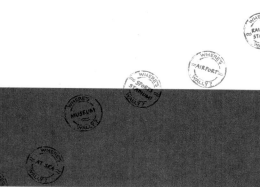

WHERE'S
WALLY?

HI FRIENDS!

MY NAME IS WALLY. I'M JUST SETTING OFF ON A WORLDWIDE HIKE. YOU CAN COME TOO. ALL YOU HAVE TO DO IS FIND ME.

I'VE GOT ALL I NEED – WALKING STICK, KETTLE, MALLET, CUP, RUCKSACK, SLEEPING BAG, BINOCULARS, CAMERA, SNORKEL, BELT, BAG AND SHOVEL.

I'M NOT TRAVELLING ON MY OWN. WHEREVER I GO, THERE ARE LOTS OF OTHER CHARACTERS FOR YOU TO SPOT. FIRST FIND WOOF (BUT ALL YOU CAN SEE IS HIS TAIL), WENDA, WIZARD WHITEBEARD AND ODLAW. THEN FIND 25 WALLY-WATCHERS SOMEWHERE, EACH OF WHOM APPEARS ONLY ONCE ON MY TRAVELS. CAN YOU FIND ONE OTHER CHARACTER WHO APPEARS IN EVERY SCENE? ALSO IN EVERY SCENE, CAN YOU SPOT MY KEY, WOOF'S BONE, WENDA'S CAMERA, WIZARD WHITEBEARD'S SCROLL, AND ODLAW'S BINOCULARS?

WOW! WHAT A SEARCH!

Wally

THE GREAT WHERE'S WALLY? CHECKLIST: PART ONE

Hundreds of things for Wally-watchers to watch out for! Don't forget PART TWO at the end of this adventure!

IN TOWN

- [ ] A dog on a roof
- [ ] A man on a fountain
- [ ] A man about to trip over a dog's lead
- [ ] A car crash
- [ ] A keen barber
- [ ] People in a street, watching television
- [ ] A puncture caused by an arrow
- [ ] A tearful tune
- [ ] A boy attacked by a plant
- [ ] A sandwich
- [ ] A waiter who isn't concentrating
- [ ] Two firemen waving at each other
- [ ] A face on a wall
- [ ] A man coming out of a man hole
- [ ] A man feeding birds

ON THE BEACH

- [ ] A dog and its owners wearing sunglasses
- [ ] A man who is overdressed
- [ ] A muscular medallion man
- [ ] A water skier
- [ ] A stripy photographer
- [ ] A punctured lilo
- [ ] A donkey who likes ice cream
- [ ] A man being squashed
- [ ] A punctured beach ball
- [ ] A human pyramid
- [ ] Three people reading newspapers
- [ ] A cowboy
- [ ] A human donkey
- [ ] A radio
- [ ] A cross-looking human stepping-stone
- [ ] A red lilo
- [ ] Age and beauty
- [ ] Two red-and-yellow umbrellas
- [ ] Two men with vests, one without
- [ ] A show-off with sandcastles
- [ ] Someone wearing braces
- [ ] A cream coloured dog
- [ ] Three protruding tongues
- [ ] Two oddly fitting hats
- [ ] Five sprinters
- [ ] A towel with a hole in it
- [ ] A punctured hovercraft
- [ ] A boy who's not allowed any ice cream
- [ ] Two caps with extra-long peaks

SKI SLOPES

- [ ] A man reading on a roof
- [ ] A flying skier
- [ ] A runaway skier
- [ ] A backward skier
- [ ] A portrait in snow
- [ ] An illegal fisherman
- [ ] Five people wearing stripy scarves
- [ ] Snow about to fall on two laughing men
- [ ] Three skiers who have hit trees
- [ ] An Alpine horn
- [ ] Two broken flagpoles
- [ ] A flag collector
- [ ] Four people in yellow-hooded tops
- [ ] A skier up a tree
- [ ] A water skier on snow
- [ ] A Yeti
- [ ] Two skiing reindeer
- [ ] A roof jumper
- [ ] Someone crashing through five skiers

CAMPSITE

- [ ] A bull in a hedge
- [ ] Bull horns
- [ ] A shark in a canal
- [ ] A bull seeing red
- [ ] A careless kick
- [ ] Tea in a lap
- [ ] A low bridge
- [ ] A person knocked over by a mallet
- [ ] A man surprised undressing
- [ ] A bicycle tyre about to be punctured
- [ ] Six dogs
- [ ] A scarecrow that doesn't work
- [ ] A wigwam
- [ ] Large biceps
- [ ] Three campers with very long beards
- [ ] A collapsed tent
- [ ] A smoking barbecue
- [ ] A fisherman catching old boots
- [ ] A winning penny-farthing
- [ ] A boy scout making fire
- [ ] A roller hiker
- [ ] A man blowing up a dinghy
- [ ] Thirsty walkers
- [ ] Runners on the road
- [ ] A bull chasing two people
- [ ] A camper's butler

THE RAILWAY STATION

- [ ] Four shovels and five spades
- [ ] A trolley carrying five suitcases
- [ ] People being knocked over by a door
- [ ] A man about to step on a ball
- [ ] Three different times at the same time
- [ ] A wheelbarrow pram
- [ ] A face on a train
- [ ] Five people reading one newspaper
- [ ] A show-off with a suitcase
- [ ] Someone tripping over a dog
- [ ] Two men with red-and-white-striped ties
- [ ] A smoking train
- [ ] A squeeze on a bench
- [ ] A dog tearing a man's trousers
- [ ] A man sitting on a suitcase
- [ ] Twenty cows
- [ ] Someone struggling to lift a suitcase
- [ ] Two suitcases spilling their contents
- [ ] A broken weighing machine

AIRPORT

- [ ] A flying saucer
- [ ] A boy sitting with the revolving luggage
- [ ] A leaking fuel pipe
- [ ] Flight controllers playing badminton
- [ ] A rocket
- [ ] A tower on top of the control tower
- [ ] Three watch smugglers
- [ ] An airport worker resting on a plane
- [ ] A forklift truck
- [ ] A wind-sock
- [ ] Someone with a bucket and spade
- [ ] Six air hostesses in light blue uniforms
- [ ] A plane with giant tail wings
- [ ] A fire engine and ten firemen
- [ ] Two passengers wearing white hats
- [ ] A plane that doesn't fly
- [ ] A flying Ace
- [ ] A pen and paper
- [ ] Runners on a runway
- [ ] Five men blowing up a balloon
- [ ] Dracula
- [ ] Three childish pilots
- [ ] Eighteen airport workers with yellow caps

HI FRIENDS!

MY NAME IS WALLY. I'M JUST SETTING OFF ON A WORLDWIDE HIKE. YOU CAN COME TOO. ALL YOU HAVE TO DO IS FIND ME.

I'VE GOT ALL I NEED – WALKING STICK, KETTLE, MALLET, CUP, RUCKSACK, SLEEPING BAG, BINOCULARS, CAMERA, SNORKEL, BELT, BAG AND SHOVEL.

I'M NOT TRAVELLING ON MY OWN. WHEREVER I GO, THERE ARE LOTS OF OTHER CHARACTERS FOR YOU TO SPOT. FIRST FIND WOOF (BUT ALL YOU CAN SEE IS HIS TAIL), WENDA, WIZARD WHITEBEARD AND ODLAW. THEN FIND 25 WALLY-WATCHERS SOMEWHERE, EACH OF WHOM APPEARS ONLY ONCE ON MY TRAVELS. CAN YOU FIND ONE OTHER CHARACTER WHO APPEARS IN EVERY SCENE? ALSO IN EVERY SCENE, CAN YOU SPOT MY KEY, WOOF'S BONE, WENDA'S CAMERA, WIZARD WHITEBEARD'S SCROLL, AND ODLAW'S BINOCULARS?

WOW! WHAT A SEARCH! Wally

GREETINGS,
WALLY FOLLOWERS!
WOW, THE BEACH WAS
GREAT TODAY! ALL
AROUND ME I SAW
STRIPES ON TOWELS,
CLOTHES, UMBRELLAS,
AND BEACH HUTS.
THERE WAS A SAND-
CASTLE WITH A REAL
KNIGHT IN ARMOUR
INSIDE! FANTASTIC!

Wally

TO:
WALLY FOLLOWERS,
HERE, THERE,
EVERYWHERE.

WHERE'S
ON THE BEACH
WALLY?

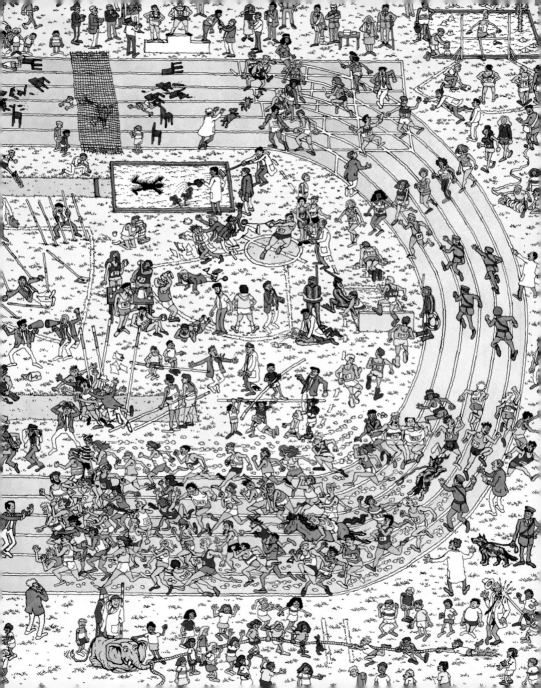

HOW-DE-DOO, WALLY SCHOLARS!
AS YOU KNOW, I LOVE TO
LEARN. SO IT'S GREAT GOING
TO MUSEUMS. TODAY I FOUND
OUT ABOUT TICKLING THE
TOES OF A MAN IN THE
STOCKS; ABOUT HOW TO FIRE
A CATAPULT; ABOUT HOW TO
MAKE A CHARIOT WORK.
NOW THAT'S LEARNING!

Wally

TO:
WALLY SCHOLARS,
AT SCHOOL,
IN CLASS,
AGAIN.

WHERE WALLY? MUSEUM

WATCH OUT, WALLY HUNTERS!
I LOVE ALL ANIMALS, THAT'S
FOR SURE. I LOVE THAT HIPPO
WITH ITS ALARM CLOCK;
THAT LION HAVING ITS MANE
COMBED; THE HAT-EATING
GIRAFFE; THE OWLS IN
SUNGLASSES. GREAT!

Wally

TO:
WALLY HUNTERS,
NICE PLACE,
THE JUNGLE,
OUTSIDE.

WHERE
SAFARI PARK
WALLY?

THE GREAT WHERE'S WALLY?
CHECKLIST: PART TWO

SPORTS STADIUM

- Three pairs of feet, sticking out of sand
- A cowboy starting races
- Hopeless hurdlers
- Record discs thrown by a discus thrower
- A shot-put juggler
- An ear trumpet
- A vaulting horse
- A runner with two wheels
- A parachuting vaulter
- A Scotsman with a caber
- An elephant pulling a rope
- People being knocked over by a hammer
- A gardener
- Three frogmen
- A runner without any shorts on
- A bed
- A bandaged boy
- A runner with four legs
- A sunken jumper
- Two athletes with stripy towels
- A boy squirting water
- Ten children taking part in the three-legged race
- An umpire chasing a dog, chasing a cat, chasing a mouse

MUSEUM

- A very big skeleton
- A clown squirting water
- A boy in a catapult
- A bird's nest in a woman's hair
- A popping bicep
- One circular portrait picture frame
- A knight watching television
- Picture robbers
- A toppling row of pots
- A highwayman
- A leaking watercolour
- Fighting pictures
- A king and queen
- A rude character inside a picture
- Three cavemen
- A lady wearing a red scarf
- Charioteers
- A collapsing pillar

AT SEA

- A windsurfer
- A rubber dinghy punctured by an arrow
- A sword fight with a swordfish
- A school of whales
- Seasick sailors
- A leaking diver
- A bathtub
- A bearded man wearing sunglasses
- A game of noughts and crosses
- A lucky fisherman
- Three lumberjacks
- Unlucky fishermen
- Two water skiers in a tangle
- A cowboy riding a seahorse
- Fish robbers
- A fishy photo
- Uninvited pirates climbing aboard ship
- A Chinese junk
- A wave at sea
- A man being strangled by an octopus
- A boat which has crashed into a safety buoy

SAFARI PARK

- Noah's Ark
- A message in a bottle
- A hippo having its teeth cleaned
- A bird's nest in an antler
- A hungry giraffe
- An ice-cream robber
- Zebras crossing a zebra crossing
- Father Christmas and a contented reindeer
- A unicorn
- Fifteen safari park rangers
- Daddy Bear, Mummy Bear and Baby Bear
- Caged people
- A lion next to the driver in a car
- Tarzan
- Lion cubs
- Two ladies with red handbags
- Two queues for the toilets
- Animals' beauty parlour
- An elephant squirting water

DEPARTMENT STORE

- A red-suited pushchair passenger
- A man whose boots face the wrong way
- A man with heavy shopping
- A misbehaving vacuum cleaner
- Ties that match their wearers
- A pram bumping into a shopper
- A boy trying on a top hat
- A man trying on a jacket that's too big
- A girl wearing a red anorak
- A boy riding in a trolley bag
- A dangerous glove that's come alive
- A shopper tripping over a ball on the floor

FAIRGROUND

- A cannon at a rifle range
- A bumper car run wild
- Ten coloured hoops
- A one-armed bandit
- A ragdoll
- Twelve uniformed fairground staff
- A runaway fairground horse
- Six birds
- A haunted house
- Seven lost children and a lost dog
- A tank crash
- Three clowns
- Three men dressed as bears

WOW! WHAT A SEARCH!

Did you find Wally, all his friends and all the things they lost? Did you find the one scene where Wally and Odlaw both lost their binoculars? Odlaw's binoculars are the ones nearest to him. Did you find the extra character who appears in every scene? If not, keep looking!
Wow! Fantastic!

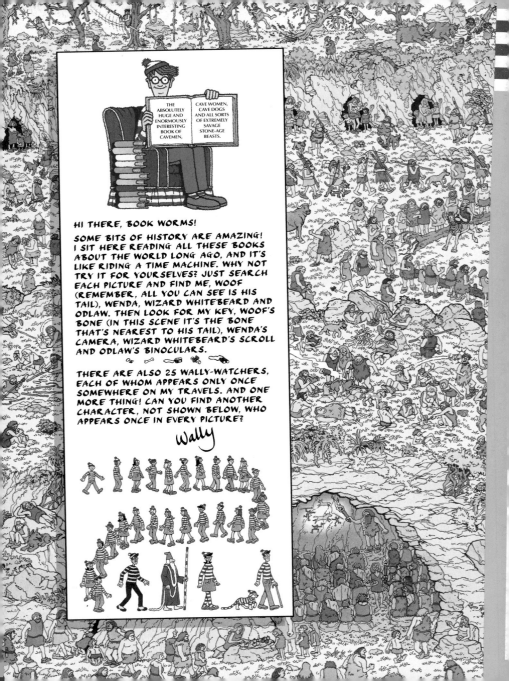

THE ABSOLUTELY HUGE AND ENORMOUSLY INTERESTING BOOK OF CAVEMEN,

CAVE WOMEN, CAVE DOGS AND ALL SORTS OF EXTREMELY SAVAGE STONE-AGE BEASTS.

HI THERE, BOOK WORMS!

SOME BITS OF HISTORY ARE AMAZING! I SIT HERE READING ALL THESE BOOKS ABOUT THE WORLD LONG AGO, AND IT'S LIKE RIDING A TIME MACHINE. WHY NOT TRY IT FOR YOURSELVES? JUST SEARCH EACH PICTURE AND FIND ME, WOOF (REMEMBER, ALL YOU CAN SEE IS HIS TAIL), WENDA, WIZARD WHITEBEARD AND ODLAW. THEN LOOK FOR MY KEY, WOOF'S BONE (IN THIS SCENE IT'S THE BONE THAT'S NEAREST TO HIS TAIL), WENDA'S CAMERA, WIZARD WHITEBEARD'S SCROLL AND ODLAW'S BINOCULARS.

THERE ARE ALSO 25 WALLY-WATCHERS, EACH OF WHOM APPEARS ONLY ONCE SOMEWHERE ON MY TRAVELS. AND ONE MORE THING! CAN YOU FIND ANOTHER CHARACTER, NOT SHOWN BELOW, WHO APPEARS ONCE IN EVERY PICTURE?

Wally

THE GREAT WHERE'S WALLY NOW? CHECKLIST: PART ONE

Hundreds more things for time travellers to look for! Don't forget PART TWO at the end of this adventure!

THE STONE AGE

- [ ] Four cavemen swinging into trouble
- [ ] An accident with an axe
- [ ] A great invention
- [ ] A Stone-Age rodeo
- [ ] Boars chasing a man
- [ ] Men chasing a boar
- [ ] Seven fish
- [ ] Romantic cavemen and cavewomen
- [ ] A mammoth squirt
- [ ] A bear trap
- [ ] A mammoth in the river
- [ ] A fruit stall
- [ ] Charging woolly rhinos
- [ ] A big cover-up
- [ ] A trunk holding a trunk
- [ ] A knock-out game of baseball
- [ ] A rocky picture show
- [ ] An upside-down boar
- [ ] A spoiled dog
- [ ] A lesson on dinosaurs
- [ ] A very scruffy family
- [ ] Some dangerous spear fishermen

THE RIDDLE OF THE PYRAMIDS

- [ ] A Pharaoh choosing a sarcophagus
- [ ] An upside-down pyramid
- [ ] A little boy helping to paint a mural
- [ ] Someone wearing a red cape
- [ ] A chariot racer without his chariot
- [ ] Men carrying a mural in a mural
- [ ] A group of posing gods
- [ ] Six workers pushing a block of stone
- [ ] Two assistants mixing paint
- [ ] Dates falling from a tree
- [ ] Stones defying gravity
- [ ] A thirsty sphinx
- [ ] A runaway block of stone
- [ ] Nine shields
- [ ] Someone blowing a horn
- [ ] A picture firing an arrow
- [ ] Three water-carriers
- [ ] Sunbathers in peril
- [ ] A messy milking session
- [ ] A contented animal being petted
- [ ] Pyramids of sand

FUN AND GAMES IN ANCIENT ROME

- [ ] A charioteer who has lost his chariot
- [ ] Coliseum cleaners
- [ ] An unequal contest with spears
- [ ] A winner who is about to lose
- [ ] A lion with good table manners
- [ ] A deadly set of wheels
- [ ] Lion cubs being teased
- [ ] Four shields that match their owners
- [ ] A leopard chasing a leopard skin
- [ ] Lions giving the paws-down
- [ ] A pyramid of lions
- [ ] A piggyback puncher
- [ ] An awful musician
- [ ] A painful fork-lift
- [ ] A horse holding the reins
- [ ] A leopard in love
- [ ] A Roman keeping score
- [ ] A gladiator losing his sandals

ON TOUR WITH THE VIKINGS

- [ ] A happy figurehead
- [ ] Figureheads in love
- [ ] A man being used as a club
- [ ] A tearful sheep
- [ ] Two hopeless hiding places
- [ ] Some childish Vikings
- [ ] Three spearheads being lopped off
- [ ] An eagle posing as a helmet
- [ ] A sailor tearing a sail
- [ ] A heavily armed Viking
- [ ] A patchy couple
- [ ] A beard with a foot on it
- [ ] A burning behind
- [ ] A bending boat
- [ ] Three startled figureheads
- [ ] Locked horns
- [ ] A helmet with a spider on it
- [ ] A helmet of smoke
- [ ] A bullfight

CHAOS AT THE CASTLE

- [ ] A soldier getting the point
- [ ] A man about to be catapulted
- [ ] A human bridge
- [ ] A key that is out of reach
- [ ] A message in a bottle
- [ ] A cauldron of boiling oil
- [ ] A battering-man
- [ ] Two hands gripping a soldier's arms
- [ ] A catapult aiming the wrong way
- [ ] Six defenders wearing red shoes
- [ ] A load of washing
- [ ] A shower of spears
- [ ] A soldier fast asleep
- [ ] A ladder that is too short
- [ ] Flattened soldiers
- [ ] Rock faces
- [ ] Attackers in the wrong colour stripes
- [ ] A ticklish situation

ONCE UPON A SATURDAY MORNING

- [ ] A dirty downpour
- [ ] Archers missing the target
- [ ] A jouster sitting back to front
- [ ] A dog stalking a cat stalking some birds
- [ ] A jouster who needs lots of practice
- [ ] A man making a bear dance
- [ ] A bear making a man dance
- [ ] Fruit and vegetable thieves
- [ ] Hats that are tied together
- [ ] A juggling jester
- [ ] A long line of pickpockets
- [ ] A very long drink
- [ ] A heavily burdened beast
- [ ] A gentleman kissing a lady's hand
- [ ] A man scything hats
- [ ] An angry fish
- [ ] A ticklish torture
- [ ] Minstrels making an awful noise

THE ABSOLUTELY HUGE AND ENORMOUSLY INTERESTING BOOK OF CAVEMEN,

CAVE WOMEN, CAVE DOGS AND ALL SORTS OF EXTREMELY SAVAGE STONE-AGE BEASTS.

HI THERE, BOOK WORMS!

SOME BITS OF HISTORY ARE AMAZING! I SIT HERE READING ALL THESE BOOKS ABOUT THE WORLD LONG AGO, AND IT'S LIKE RIDING A TIME MACHINE. WHY NOT TRY IT FOR YOURSELVES? JUST SEARCH EACH PICTURE AND FIND ME, WOOF (REMEMBER, ALL YOU CAN SEE IS HIS TAIL), WENDA, WIZARD WHITEBEARD AND ODLAW. THEN LOOK FOR MY KEY, WOOF'S BONE (IN THIS SCENE IT'S THE BONE THAT'S NEAREST TO HIS TAIL), WENDA'S CAMERA, WIZARD WHITEBEARD'S SCROLL AND ODLAW'S BINOCULARS.

THERE ARE ALSO 25 WALLY-WATCHERS, EACH OF WHOM APPEARS ONLY ONCE SOMEWHERE ON MY TRAVELS. AND ONE MORE THING! CAN YOU FIND ANOTHER CHARACTER, NOT SHOWN BELOW, WHO APPEARS ONCE IN EVERY PICTURE?

Wally

4,578 YEARS AGO

THE RIDDLE OF THE PYRAMIDS

THE ANCIENT EGYPTIANS WERE VERY CLEVER PEOPLE WHO LOVED GOATS, CATS AND SPHINXES, AND INVENTED PYRAMIDS. WITH GREAT SKILL AND HARD WORK THEY BUILT HUGE WONDERS IN THE DESERT.

BUT FOR HUNDREDS OF YEARS MANY PEOPLE WERE PUZZLED BY THEM. WHAT WERE THEY FOR? WHY WERE THEY SO BIG?

WHY WERE THEY THAT SHAPE? WAS IT POSSIBLE (OR EVEN LIKELY) THAT PHARAOHS WERE BURIED UNDER THEM? THESE MAGNIFICENT MONUMENTS ARE STILL AMAZING PEOPLE TO THIS DAY.

2,000 YEARS AGO

FVN AND GAMES IN ANCIENT ROME

THE ROMANS SPENT MOST OF THEIR TIME FIGHTING, CONQVERING, LEARNING LATIN AND MAKING ROADS. WHEN THEY TOOK THEIR HOLIDAYS THEY ALWAYS HAD GAMES AT THE COLISEVM (AN OLD SORT OF PLAYGROVND). THEIR FAVOVRITE GAMES WERE FIGHTING, MORE FIGHTING, CHARIOT RACING, FIGHTING AND FEEDING CHRISTIANS TO LIONS. WHEN THE CROWD GAVE A GLADIATOR THE THVMBS DOWN, IT MEANT KILL YOVR OPPONENT. THVMBS VP MEANT LET HIM GO, TO FIGHT TO THE DEATH ANOTHER DAY.

1,003 YEARS AGO

ON TOUR WITH THE VIKINGS

At home the Vikings were quiet people, who liked knitting and cheese tasting and boring things like that. But on tour they went wild. They put on their best horned hats and sailed across the sea, singing and shouting like mad. If you heard them coming, it was best to run away because once they had arrived and unpacked their axes, there was no holding them back.

800 YEARS AGO

Chaos at the Castle

Castles were built all across Europe and the people living in them often had a beautiful view of the countryside. Unfortunately they might also have had a view of an army laying siege to their castle. Luckily when these besieging armies finally ran out of clean tights and tunics they returned home. For years afterwards the knights told stories of the spectacular castles they had battered and bashed and the fascinating people they had captured — and wondered why they were never invited to parties!

600 YEARS AGO

ONCE UPON A SATURDAY MORNING

The Middle Ages were a very merry time to be alive, especially on Saturdays, as long as you didn't get caught. Short skirts and stripy tights were in fashion for men; everybody knew lots of jokes; there was widespread juggling and jousting and archery and jesting and fun. But if you got into trouble, the Middle Ages could be miserable. For the man in the stocks or the pillory or about to lose his head, Saturday morning was no laughing matter.

171,185 DAYS AGO

THE LAST DAYS OF THE AZTECS

The Aztecs lived in sunny Mexico and were rich and strong and liked swinging from poles pretending to be eagles. They also liked making human sacrifices to their gods, so it was best to agree with everything they said. The Spanish were also rich and strong, and some of them, called conquistadors, came to Mexico in 1519 to have an adventure.

However, when the Aztecs and Spanish met they did not agree on much.

400 YEARS AGO

Is red better than blue? What do you mean, your poem about cherry blossom is better than mine? Shall we have another cup of tea? Over difficult questions such as these, the Japanese fought fiercely for hundreds of years. The fiercest fighters of all were the samurai, who wore flags on their backs so that their mummies could find them. The fighters without flags were called ashigaru. They couldn't take a joke any better than the samurai, especially about not having flags.

TROUBLE IN OLD JAPAN

250 YEARS AGO

BEING A PIRATE

(Shiver-me-timbers!)

It was really a lot of fun being a pirate, especially if you were very hairy and didn't have much in the way of brains. It also helped if you had a peg-leg, an eye patch, a bandana and had a pirate's hat with your name-tag sewn inside and a treasure-map and a rusty cutlass. Once there were lots of pirates, but they died out in the end because too many of them were men (which is not a good idea).

HAVING A BALL IN GAYE PAREE

The history of France has some very bad bits, like getting your head chopped off by Madame Guillotine in the French Revolution; and some very good bits, like the invention of smelly cheese. In 1870 Napoleon (the third one) threw a marvellous ball in Paris to celebrate 1870 being a good bit. All the beautiful people came and danced the night away to a band called the Third Republic.

100 YEARS AGO
THE GOLD RUSH

At the end of the 19th century large numbers of excited **AMERICANS** were frequently to be seen **RUSHING** headlong towards **HOLES** in the ground, hoping to find **GOLD**. Most of them never even found the holes in the ground. But at least they had a **GOOD DAY**, with plenty of **EXERCISE** and **FRESH AIR**, which kept them **HEALTHY**. And health is much more valuable than **GOLD** . . . well, nearly more valuable . . . isn't it?

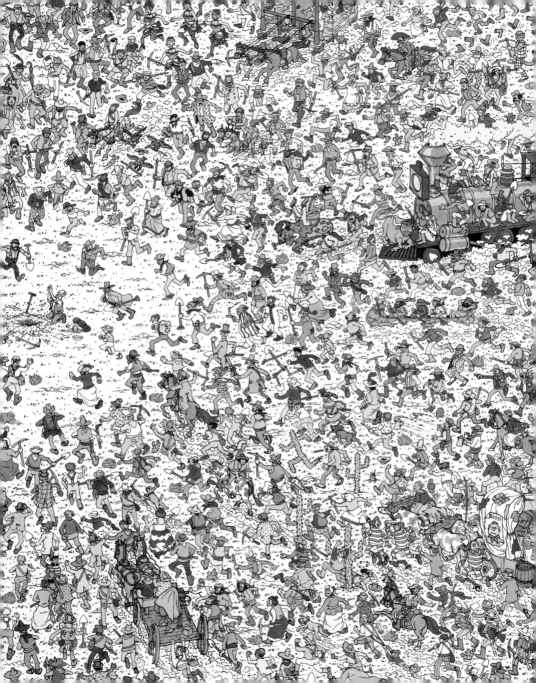

THE GREAT WHERE'S WALLY NOW?
CHECKLIST: PART TWO

THE LAST DAYS OF THE AZTECS

- A tall headdress
- Aztecs in a spin
- A conquistador with his fingers in his ears
- Three archers causing one man pain
- A picture looking sideways
- A tussle for a flag
- Shocked faces staring at a cannonball
- A drummer perched on high
- A human missile
- A frightened horse
- Yellow teeth
- A kissing conquistador
- Eagles diving to attack
- A boy robbing a robber
- An Aztec ball game
- A bouncing slingshot

TROUBLE IN OLD JAPAN

- Three warriors trapped on a bridge
- Warriors with daggers in their mouths
- Nine warriors holding clubs
- A sword being cut in two
- A warrior bending over backwards
- A wrestler out for the count
- A warrior holding a broken spear
- Warriors making a splash
- Warriors running under a bridge
- An easily scared horse
- A downtrodden warrior
- Two gangs of arrow thieves
- A shot under a hat
- A flag full of arrows
- A spear thrown backwards

BEING A PIRATE

- A woman waving a sword
- A big pushover
- A pirate being pinched by a crab
- A pirate firing from a palm tree
- A backfiring blunderbuss
- A pirate with four pistols and a sword
- Sharks ready to eat
- A skull with an eye patch
- A feeble cannon shot
- Feet sticking out of a cannon
- A flattered ship's figurehead
- A three-way clubbing
- A winking skull
- A creature with eight arms
- A crow's nest
- A cannonball puncher
- A deadly handshake
- A boat in a bathtub
- An empty treasure chest
- A cargo of heavyweights
- A human surfboard

HAVING A BALL IN GAYE PAREE

- Cancan dancers
- Two musicians fighting with their bows
- A man weighed down by his medals
- Two women hiding behind fans
- A man about to get a crashing headache
- A tall man with a short woman
- A man caught by a statue
- Guests swinging from the chandeliers
- A man playing his bow with a violin
- A waiter spilling wine
- A heavy pair of trousers
- A scruffy man
- An odd assortment of weapons
- A man wearing a pile of hats
- An insolent statue
- A dangerous dancer
- A harpist firing an arrow
- A woman losing her dress

THE GOLD RUSH

- An overloaded donkey
- A running cactus
- A man being dragged by his horse
- Running boots
- Running tools
- A man falling over a barrel
- A dog taking his pick
- A train that has come off the rails
- A canoe out of water
- A clown on a unicycle
- A man on a buffalo
- Prospecting vultures
- Three escaped convicts
- A man running into a cactus
- A moving house
- A man on a penny farthing
- Men in their night clothes
- A man being dragged by his dog
- Prospecting snakes
- A man taking a photograph
- A horse wearing a hat

THE FUTURE

- A smiling satellite
- Mercury
- Hitch-hikers in the Galaxy
- Spaceships on a collision course
- A robot and his dog
- An alien holding six drinks
- Humans laughing at an alien
- Two smiling robots walking together
- Saturn being sat on
- Three robot waiters
- Space traffic lights
- A biplane
- Aliens laughing at humans
- A crash landing
- The Great Bear
- Costumes from every page of this book
- Flying saucers
- Neptune
- The Milky Way
- A brown volleyball
- A blue alien with a hand in its pocket

WHAT A MYSTERY!

Wow, Wally-watchers! As well as finding Wally and his friends, did you find all the things they lost? Did you find the mystery character in every picture?
It may be difficult, but keep searching and eventually you'll find her (now, that's a clue!). And one last thing: somewhere one of the
Wally-watchers lost the bobble from his hat. Can you spot which one and find the bobble?

WHERE'S
WALLY?
THE
FANTASTIC
JOURNEY

THE GOBBLING GLUTTONS

ONCE UPON A TIME WALLY
EMBARKED UPON A FANTASTIC
JOURNEY. FIRST, AMONG A
THRONG OF GOBBLING GLUTTONS,
HE MET WIZARD WHITEBEARD, WHO
COMMANDED HIM TO FIND A SCROLL AND
THEN TO FIND ANOTHER AT EVERY STAGE OF
HIS JOURNEY, FOR WHEN HE HAD FOUND
12 SCROLLS, HE WOULD UNDERSTAND THE
TRUTH ABOUT HIMSELF.

IN EVERY PICTURE FIND WALLY, WOOF (BUT ALL
YOU CAN SEE IS HIS TAIL), WENDA, WIZARD
WHITEBEARD, ODLAW AND THE SCROLL. THEN
FIND WALLY'S KEY, WOOF'S BONE (IN THIS SCENE
IT'S THE BONE THAT'S NEAREST TO HIS TAIL),
WENDA'S CAMERA AND ODLAW'S BINOCULARS.

THERE ARE ALSO 25 WALLY-WATCHERS, EACH OF
WHOM APPEARS ONLY ONCE SOMEWHERE IN
THE FOLLOWING 12 PICTURES. AND ONE MORE
THING! CAN YOU FIND ANOTHER CHARACTER,
NOT SHOWN BELOW, WHO APPEARS ONCE IN
EVERY PICTURE EXCEPT THE LAST?

THE GREAT WHERE'S WALLY? THE FANTASTIC JOURNEY CHECKLIST: PART ONE

Hundreds more things for Wally followers to look for! Don't forget PART TWO at the end of this adventure!

THE GOBBLING GLUTTONS

- [ ] A strong waiter and a weak one
- [ ] Long-distance smells
- [ ] Unequal portions of pie
- [ ] A man who has had too much to drink
- [ ] People who are going the wrong way
- [ ] Very tough dishes
- [ ] An upside-down dish
- [ ] Knights drinking through straws
- [ ] A very hot dinner
- [ ] A clever drink-pourer
- [ ] Giant sausages
- [ ] A custard fight
- [ ] An overloaded seat
- [ ] Beard-flavoured soup
- [ ] Men pulling legs
- [ ] A painful spillage
- [ ] A man tied up in spaghetti
- [ ] A knock-out dish
- [ ] A man who has eaten too much
- [ ] A tall diner eating a tall dish
- [ ] An exploding pie
- [ ] A giant sausage breaking in half
- [ ] A smell travelling through two people
- [ ] A bear shield

THE BATTLING MONKS

- [ ] Two fire engines
- [ ] Hot-footed monks
- [ ] A bridge made of monks
- [ ] A cheeky monk
- [ ] A diving monk
- [ ] A scared statue
- [ ] Fire meeting water
- [ ] A snaking jet of water
- [ ] Chasers being chased
- [ ] A smug statue
- [ ] A snaking jet of flame
- [ ] A five-way wash-out
- [ ] A burning bridge
- [ ] Seven burning backsides
- [ ] Monks worshipping the Flowing Bucket of Water
- [ ] Monks shielding themselves from lava
- [ ] Thirteen trapped and extremely worried monks
- [ ] A monk seeing an oncoming jet of flame
- [ ] Monks worshipping the Mighty Erupting Volcano
- [ ] A very worried monk confronted by two opponents
- [ ] A burning hose
- [ ] Monks and lava pouring out of a volcano
- [ ] A chain of water
- [ ] Two monks accidentally attacking their brothers

THE DRAGON FLYERS

- [ ] Two dragons on a collision course
- [ ] A pedestrian crossing
- [ ] Two hangers-on
- [ ] Four hitchhikers
- [ ] Salesmen selling young dragons
- [ ] Dragon flyer highwaymen
- [ ] A concussed dragon
- [ ] Dragon cops and robbers
- [ ] Upside-down flyers
- [ ] A dragon beauty parlour
- [ ] A flying tower
- [ ] A dragon-tail staircase
- [ ] A topsy-turvy tower
- [ ] Dragons in love
- [ ] Flyers with dragon-tail-shaped beards
- [ ] Five extra-long red bus dragons
- [ ] A tail fight
- [ ] A passenger with empty pockets
- [ ] Queues at three bus dragon stops
- [ ] One person wearing two red shoes
- [ ] A dragon flying backwards
- [ ] A dragon indoors
- [ ] Two suddenly dragonless riders

THE GREAT BALL-GAME PLAYERS

- [ ] A three-way drink
- [ ] A chase that goes round in circles
- [ ] A backside shot
- [ ] A spectator surrounded by three rival supporters
- [ ] A row of hand-held banners
- [ ] Two tall players versus short ones
- [ ] A shot that breaks the woodwork
- [ ] A mob chasing a player backwards
- [ ] Players who are digging for victory
- [ ] A face about to hit a fist
- [ ] Seven awful singers
- [ ] A face made of balls
- [ ] A player chasing a mob
- [ ] Players pulling each other's hoods
- [ ] A flag with a hole in it
- [ ] A mob of players all holding balls
- [ ] A player heading a ball
- [ ] A player tripping over a rock
- [ ] A player punching a ball
- [ ] A spectator accidentally hitting two others
- [ ] A player poking his tongue out at a mob
- [ ] A mouth pulled open by a beard
- [ ] Players who can't see where they are going

THE FEROCIOUS RED DWARFS

- [ ] A spear-breaking slingshot
- [ ] Two punches causing chain reactions
- [ ] Fat and thin spears and spearmen
- [ ] A spearman being knocked through a flag
- [ ] A collar made out of a shield
- [ ] A prison made of spears
- [ ] A spearman trapped by his battle dress
- [ ] An axe-head causing headaches
- [ ] Dwarves disguised as spearmen
- [ ] Opponents charging through each other
- [ ] A spearman running away from a spear
- [ ] A sneaky spear-bender
- [ ] A devious disarmer
- [ ] A dwarf who is on the wrong side
- [ ] Cheeky target practice
- [ ] A stick-up machine
- [ ] Tangled spears
- [ ] A slingshot causing a chain reaction
- [ ] A sword cutting through a shield
- [ ] A spear hitting a spearman's shield
- [ ] A dwarf hiding up a spear
- [ ] A spear knocking off a dwarf's helmet
- [ ] Spearmen who have jumped out of their clothes

THE NASTY NASTIES

- [ ] A vampire who is scared of ghosts
- [ ] A dancing mummy
- [ ] Vampires drinking through straws
- [ ] Gargoyle lovers
- [ ] An upside-down torture
- [ ] A baseball bat
- [ ] Three wolfmen
- [ ] A mummy who is coming undone
- [ ] Dog, cat and mouse doorways
- [ ] A vampire mirror test
- [ ] A frightened skeleton
- [ ] Courting cats
- [ ] A ghoulish game of skittles
- [ ] A gargoyle being poked on the nose
- [ ] An upside-down gargoyle
- [ ] Fang-tastic flight controllers
- [ ] Three witches flying backwards
- [ ] A witch losing her broomstick
- [ ] A broomstick flying a witch
- [ ] A ticklish torture
- [ ] A vampire about to get the chop
- [ ] A ghost train
- [ ] A vampire who doesn't fit his coffin
- [ ] A three-eyed, hooded torturer

THE GOBBLING GLUTTONS

ONCE UPON A TIME WALLY
EMBARKED UPON A FANTASTIC
JOURNEY. FIRST, AMONG A
THRONG OF GOBBLING GLUTTONS,
HE MET WIZARD WHITEBEARD, WHO
COMMANDED HIM TO FIND A SCROLL AND
THEN TO FIND ANOTHER AT EVERY STAGE OF
HIS JOURNEY, FOR WHEN HE HAD FOUND
12 SCROLLS, HE WOULD UNDERSTAND THE
TRUTH ABOUT HIMSELF.

IN EVERY PICTURE FIND WALLY, WOOF (BUT ALL
YOU CAN SEE IS HIS TAIL), WENDA, WIZARD
WHITEBEARD, ODLAW AND THE SCROLL. THEN
FIND WALLY'S KEY, WOOF'S BONE (IN THIS SCENE
IT'S THE BONE THAT'S NEAREST TO HIS TAIL),
WENDA'S CAMERA AND ODLAW'S BINOCULARS.

THERE ARE ALSO 25 WALLY-WATCHERS, EACH OF
WHOM APPEARS ONLY ONCE SOMEWHERE IN
THE FOLLOWING 12 PICTURES. AND ONE MORE
THING! CAN YOU FIND ANOTHER CHARACTER,
NOT SHOWN BELOW, WHO APPEARS ONCE IN
EVERY PICTURE EXCEPT THE LAST?

THE BATTLING MONKS

THEN WALLY AND WIZARD WHITEBEARD CAME
TO THE PLACE WHERE THE INVISIBLE MONKS
OF FIRE FOUGHT THE MONKS OF WATER. AND
AS WALLY SEARCHED FOR THE SECOND SCROLL,
HE SAW THAT MANY WALLIES HAD BEEN THIS WAY BEFORE.
AND WHEN HE FOUND THE SCROLL, IT WAS TIME TO
CONTINUE WITH HIS JOURNEY.

THE DRAGON FLYERS

THEN WALLY AND WIZARD WHITEBEARD CAME TO THE LAND OF THE DRAGON FLYERS, WHERE MANY WALLIES HAD BEEN BEFORE. AND WALLY SAW A COLOURFUL FLEET OF DRAGONS AND FLYERS WEARING DRAGON-TAIL HOODS FILLING THE SKY. THERE ARE ARROW SHAPES APLENTY TO SPOT IN THIS TALE OF TAILS. OH BRAINY DRAGON WATCHERS. AND WHEN WALLY FOUND THE THIRD SCROLL, IT WAS TIME TO CONTINUE HIS JOURNEY.

THE GREAT BALL-GAME PLAYERS

THEN WALLY AND WIZARD WHITEBEARD CAME TO
THE PLAYING FIELD OF THE GREAT BALL-GAME
PLAYERS, WHERE MANY WALLIES HAD BEEN BEFORE.
AND WALLY SAW THAT FOUR TEAMS WERE PLAYING AGAINST
EACH OTHER (BUT WAS ANYONE WINNING? WHAT WAS THE
SCORE? CAN YOU WORK OUT THE RULES?). THEN WALLY FOUND
THE FOURTH SCROLL AND CONTINUED WITH HIS JOURNEY.

THE FEROCIOUS RED DWARVES

THEN WALLY AND WIZARD WHITEBEARD
CAME AMONG THE FEROCIOUS RED DWARVES,
WHERE MANY WALLIES HAD BEEN BEFORE.
AND THE DWARVES WERE ATTACKING THE MANY-
COLOURED SPEARMEN, CAUSING MIGHTY MAYHEM AND
HORRID HAVOC. AND WALLY FOUND THE FIFTH SCROLL
AND CONTINUED WITH HIS JOURNEY.

THE NASTY NASTIES

THEN WALLY AND WIZARD WHITEBEARD
CAME TO THE CASTLE OF THE NASTY NASTIES,
WHERE MANY WALLIES HAD BEEN BEFORE. AND
WHEREVER WALLY WALKED, THERE WAS A CLATTERING
OF BONES (WOOF'S BONE IN THIS SCENE IS THE NEAREST TO
HIS TAIL) AND A FOUL SLURPING OF FILTHY FOOD. AND WALLY
FOUND THE SIXTH SCROLL AND CONTINUED WITH HIS JOURNEY.

THE FIGHTING FORESTERS

THEN WALLY AND WIZARD WHITEBEARD CAME
AMONG THE FIGHTING FORESTERS, WHERE
MANY WALLIES HAD BEEN BEFORE. AND IN
THEIR BATTLE WITH THE EVIL BLACK KNIGHTS, THE
FOREST WOMEN WERE AIDED BY THE ANIMALS, BY THE LIVING
MUD, EVEN BY THE TREES THEMSELVES. AND WALLY FOUND THE
SEVENTH SCROLL AND CONTINUED WITH HIS JOURNEY.

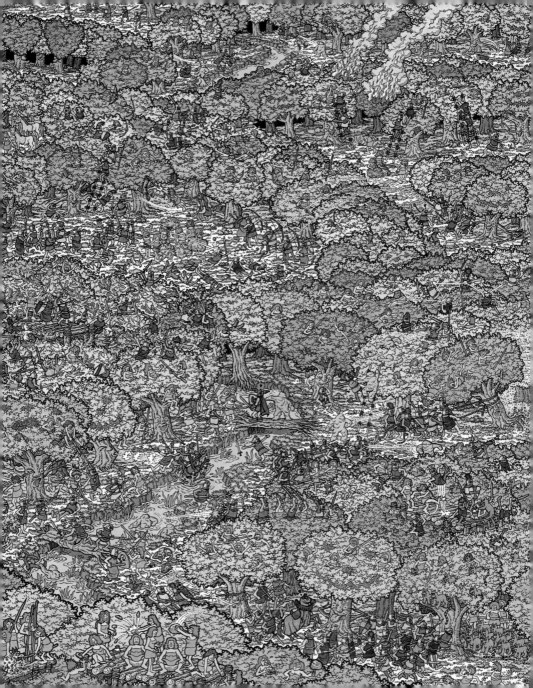

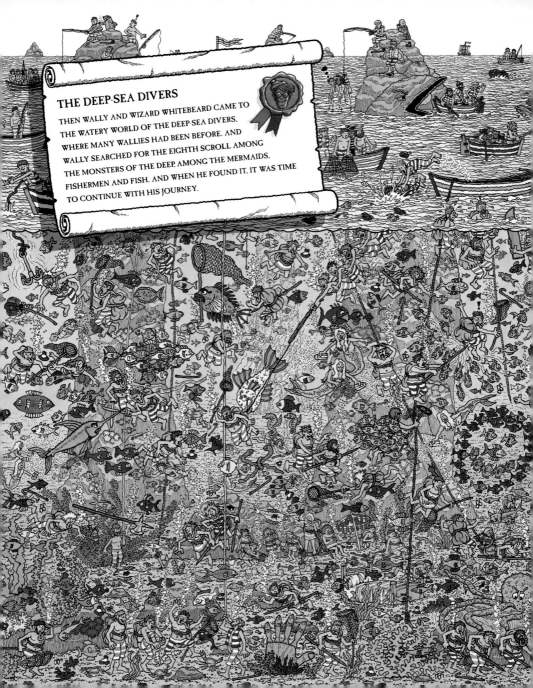

THE DEEP-SEA DIVERS

THEN WALLY AND WIZARD WHITEBEARD CAME TO
THE WATERY WORLD OF THE DEEP-SEA DIVERS,
WHERE MANY WALLIES HAD BEEN BEFORE. AND
WALLY SEARCHED FOR THE EIGHTH SCROLL AMONG
THE MONSTERS OF THE DEEP, AMONG THE MERMAIDS,
FISHERMEN AND FISH. AND WHEN HE FOUND IT, IT WAS TIME
TO CONTINUE WITH HIS JOURNEY.

THE KNIGHTS OF THE MAGIC FLAG

THEN WALLY AND WIZARD WHITEBEARD CAME
TO A PLACE MORE CROWDED THAN ANY WALLY
HAD SEEN BEFORE, WHERE TWO ARMIES WITH
MANY MAGIC FLAGS WERE LOCKED IN COMBAT.
AND WALLY SAW THAT MANY WALLIES HAD BEEN THIS WAY
BEFORE. AND WHEN HE FOUND THE NINTH SCROLL, IT WAS
TIME TO CONTINUE WITH HIS JOURNEY.

THE UNFRIENDLY GIANTS

THEN WALLY AND WIZARD WHITEBEARD CAME
TO THE LAND OF THE UNFRIENDLY GIANTS,
WHERE MANY WALLIES HAD BEEN BEFORE, AND
WALLY SAW THAT THE GIANTS WERE HORRIDLY
HARASSING THE LITTLE PEOPLE. AND WHEN HE FOUND THE
TENTH SCROLL, IT WAS TIME TO CONTINUE WITH HIS JOURNEY.

THE UNDERGROUND HUNTERS

THEN WALLY AND WIZARD WHITEBEARD CAME
AMONG THE UNDERGROUND HUNTERS, WHERE
MANY WALLIES HAD BEEN BEFORE. AND THERE
WAS MUCH MENACE IN THIS PLACE, AND A
MULTITUDE OF MALEVOLENT MONSTERS. AND
WALLY FOUND THE ELEVENTH SCROLL AND CONTINUED
WITH HIS JOURNEY.

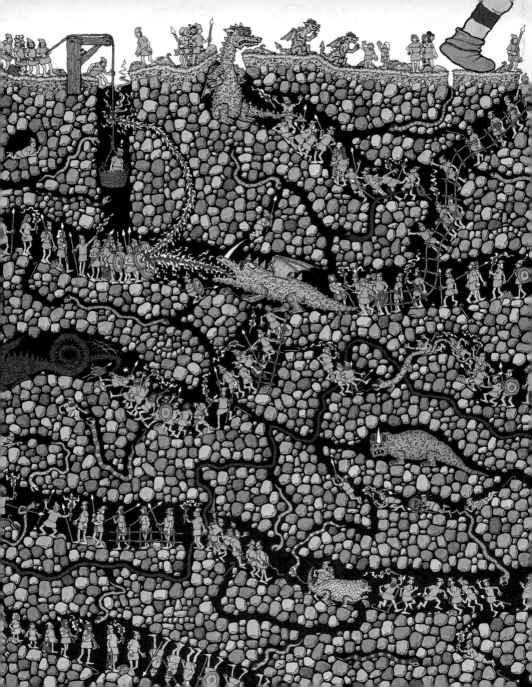

THE LAND OF WALLIES

THEN WALLY FOUND THE TWELFTH SCROLL AND SAW THE TRUTH ABOUT HIMSELF, THAT HE WAS JUST ONE WALLY AMONG MANY. HE SAW TOO THAT WALLIES OFTEN LOSE THINGS, FOR HE HIMSELF HAD LOST ONE SHOE. AND AS HE LOOKED FOR HIS SHOE, HE DISCOVERED THAT WIZARD WHITEBEARD WAS NOT HIS ONLY FELLOW TRAVELLER. THERE WERE NOW ELEVEN OTHERS – ONE FROM EVERY PLACE HE HAD BEEN TO – WHO HAD JOINED HIM ONE BY ONE ALONG THE WAY. SO NOW (OH LOYAL FOLLOWERS OF WALLY!) FIND THE REAL WALLY AND HELP HIM FIND HIS MISSING SHOE. AND THERE, IN THE LAND OF WALLIES, MAY WALLY LIVE HAPPILY EVER AFTER.

WHERE'S WALLY?
IN
HOLLYWOOD

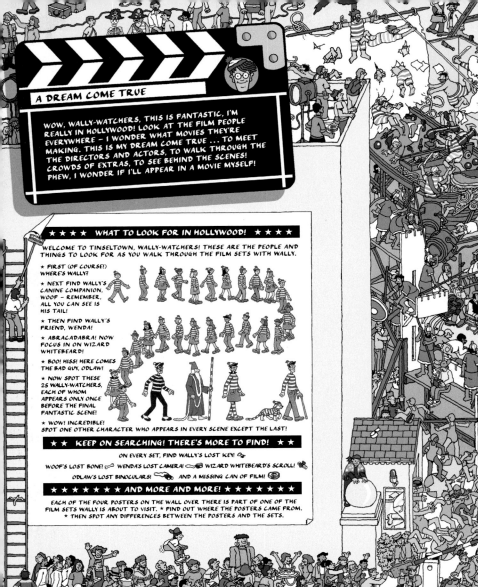

A DREAM COME TRUE

WOW, WALLY-WATCHERS, THIS IS FANTASTIC, I'M REALLY IN HOLLYWOOD! LOOK AT THE FILM PEOPLE EVERYWHERE – I WONDER WHAT MOVIES THEY'RE MAKING. THIS IS MY DREAM COME TRUE ... TO MEET THE DIRECTORS AND ACTORS, TO WALK THROUGH THE CROWDS OF EXTRAS, TO SEE BEHIND THE SCENES! PHEW, I WONDER IF I'LL APPEAR IN A MOVIE MYSELF!

★ ★ ★ ★   WHAT TO LOOK FOR IN HOLLYWOOD!   ★ ★ ★ ★

WELCOME TO TINSELTOWN, WALLY-WATCHERS! THESE ARE THE PEOPLE AND THINGS TO LOOK FOR AS YOU WALK THROUGH THE FILM SETS WITH WALLY.

★ FIRST (OF COURSE!) WHERE'S WALLY?

★ NEXT FIND WALLY'S CANINE COMPANION, WOOF – REMEMBER, ALL YOU CAN SEE IS HIS TAIL!

★ THEN FIND WALLY'S FRIEND, WENDA!

★ ABRACADABRA! NOW FOCUS IN ON WIZARD WHITEBEARD!

★ BOO! HISS! HERE COMES THE BAD GUY, ODLAW!

★ NOW SPOT THESE 25 WALLY-WATCHERS, EACH OF WHOM APPEARS ONLY ONCE BEFORE THE FINAL FANTASTIC SCENE!

★ WOW! INCREDIBLE! SPOT ONE OTHER CHARACTER WHO APPEARS IN EVERY SCENE EXCEPT THE LAST!

★ ★   KEEP ON SEARCHING! THERE'S MORE TO FIND!   ★ ★

ON EVERY SET, FIND WALLY'S LOST KEY!

WOOF'S LOST BONE!   WENDA'S LOST CAMERA!   WIZARD WHITEBEARD'S SCROLL!

ODLAW'S LOST BINOCULARS!   AND A MISSING CAN OF FILM!

★ ★ ★ ★ ★ ★ AND MORE AND MORE! ★ ★ ★ ★ ★ ★ ★

EACH OF THE FOUR POSTERS ON THE WALL OVER THERE IS PART OF ONE OF THE FILM SETS WALLY IS ABOUT TO VISIT. ★ FIND OUT WHERE THE POSTERS CAME FROM. ★ THEN SPOT ANY DIFFERENCES BETWEEN THE POSTERS AND THE SETS.

THE GREAT WHERE'S WALLY? IN HOLLYWOOD CHECKLIST: PART ONE

Lots more things for Wally-watchers to look for! Don't forget PART TWO at the end of this adventure!

★ ★ ★ A DREAM COME TRUE ★ ★ ★

- A soldier capturing a sandwich
- A double agent in a spy film
- A girl in a swimsuit with a yellow hat
- Eight pieces of heart-shaped film equipment
- A green star on a yellow ball
- A wind machine blowing out of control
- A romantic scene
- Someone walking tall
- A swing band
- Three shields
- Twenty-one pirates in striped clothing
- Ten studio security guards
- Someone who has put their foot in it
- Three people with skis
- A scenic painter
- A man wearing a spotted bow tie
- A friendly pirate

★ ★ SHHH! THIS IS A SILENT MOVIE ★ ★

- A trail of leaking buckets
- A knotted hose
- A tug-of-war
- Some flowers being watered
- A man in plus-four trousers
- Two butterfly catchers
- Nine four-legged animals
- A runaway wheel
- Seven loudhailers
- A watchtower
- Thirteen balloons
- Fifteen movie cameras
- A searchlight
- Three men tripping on some fruit
- A hose cut by an axe
- Four fire chiefs wearing peaked caps
- A railway-track ladder
- Three men wearing red shirts and braces
- Two umbrellas

★ ★ ★ HORSEPLAY IN TROY ★ ★ ★

- Five blue soldiers with red-crested helmets
- Three soldiers with extra-long cloaks
- Thirteen real four-legged animals
- Three film crew members wearing sunglasses
- Five red soldiers with blue-crested helmets
- Five yellow soldiers with blue-crested helmets
- Two statues waving at each other
- A litter bin
- Two soldiers with slings
- A soldier with a square shield
- Crew members surrendering
- Three Trojans drinking coffee
- Ten arrows that are stuck in shields
- One soldier wearing sandals
- Soldiers arguing about the time
- Some ancient traffic police
- Five soldiers with brooms

★ ★ FUN IN THE FOREIGN LEGION ★ ★

- Five men wearing vests and shorts
- A French flag with colours in the wrong order
- A modern aeroplane ruining a camera shot
- Four trees surrendering
- A rock hitting sixteen people
- Two men being shaken out of a tree
- The right costumes in the wrong colours
- A delivery of sand
- Thirteen camels
- Some date trees
- Some enemies fighting back to back
- An unpopular musician
- A man reading a book
- Three men hiding underneath animals
- An animal treading on a man's foot
- A man surrendering to a shovel
- A horseman riding in the wrong direction

★ A TREMENDOUS SONG AND DANCE ★

- One dancer wearing a blue carnation
- Some tap dancers
- A "grand" piano
- A musician playing a double bass
- Dancers wearing top hats and tails
- Sailors saluting the ship's "N" sign
- Sailors with bell-bottom trousers
- The captain's log
- A vice admiral
- A piano keyboard
- Four orange feathers
- A soldier on the wrong set
- Five real anchors
- An octopus, a shark and a fish
- Nine mops
- Four sailors with tattoos

★ CAVE OF THE PLUNDERING PIRATES ★

- A man asleep in bed
- A man awake in bed
- A pirate carrying a grey treasure chest
- A pirate wearing a blue shoe and a white shoe
- A pirate wearing a red shoe and a pink shoe
- A pirate with a red star on his cap
- A pirate with jewels in his beard
- A golden bath
- A snake
- Two dogs and a horse
- A "chest" of drawers
- Three real pirate ghosts
- A pirate barber
- Surprised miners
- Two careless carpet-carriers
- Pirates stealing camera equipment
- A pirate wearing a yellow cap

★ ★ ★ THE WILD, WILD WEST ★ ★ ★

- Two cowboys about to draw against each other
- Drinkers raising their glasses to a lady
- Outlaws holding up a stagecoach
- Some boisterous cowboys painting the town red
- Doc holiday
- The film wardrobe department
- Buffalo Bill
- The loan ranger
- Gamblers playing cards
- A couple of gunslingers
- Calamity Jane
- A buffalo **stamp**ede
- A spaghetti western
- A horse-drawn wagon
- Billy the kid
- Townspeople saluting General Store
- A band of outlaws
- Two cowboys shouting, "This town ain't big enough for the both of us."

A DREAM COME TRUE

WOW, WALLY-WATCHERS, THIS IS FANTASTIC, I'M REALLY IN HOLLYWOOD! LOOK AT THE FILM PEOPLE EVERYWHERE — I WONDER WHAT MOVIES THEY'RE MAKING. THIS IS MY DREAM COME TRUE ... TO MEET THE DIRECTORS AND ACTORS, TO WALK THROUGH THE CROWDS OF EXTRAS, TO SEE BEHIND THE SCENES! PHEW, I WONDER IF I'LL APPEAR IN A MOVIE MYSELF!

★ ★ ★ ★ WHAT TO LOOK FOR IN HOLLYWOOD! ★ ★ ★ ★

WELCOME TO TINSELTOWN, WALLY-WATCHERS! THESE ARE THE PEOPLE AND THINGS TO LOOK FOR AS YOU WALK THROUGH THE FILM SETS WITH WALLY.

★ FIRST (OF COURSE!) WHERE'S WALLY?

★ NEXT FIND WALLY'S CANINE COMPANION, WOOF — REMEMBER, ALL YOU CAN SEE IS HIS TAIL!

★ THEN FIND WALLY'S FRIEND, WENDA!

★ ABRACADABRA! NOW FOCUS IN ON WIZARD WHITEBEARD!

★ BOO! HISS! HERE COMES THE BAD GUY, ODLAW!

★ NOW SPOT THESE 25 WALLY-WATCHERS, EACH OF WHOM APPEARS ONLY ONCE BEFORE THE FINAL FANTASTIC SCENE!

★ WOW! INCREDIBLE!
SPOT ONE OTHER CHARACTER WHO APPEARS IN EVERY SCENE EXCEPT THE LAST!

★ ★ KEEP ON SEARCHING! THERE'S MORE TO FIND! ★ ★

ON EVERY SET, FIND WALLY'S LOST KEY!

WOOF'S LOST BONE!   WENDA'S LOST CAMERA!   WIZARD WHITEBEARD'S SCROLL!
ODLAW'S LOST BINOCULARS!   AND A MISSING CAN OF FILM!

★ ★ ★ ★ ★ AND MORE AND MORE! ★ ★ ★ ★ ★

EACH OF THE FOUR POSTERS ON THE WALL OVER THERE IS PART OF ONE OF THE FILM SETS WALLY IS ABOUT TO VISIT. ★ FIND OUT WHERE THE POSTERS CAME FROM. ★ THEN SPOT ANY DIFFERENCES BETWEEN THE POSTERS AND THE SETS.

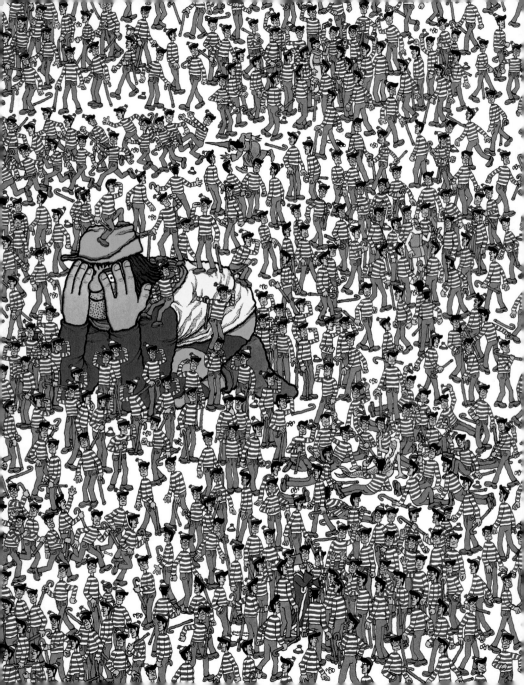

THE GREAT WHERE'S WALLY?
THE FANTASTIC JOURNEY CHECKLIST: PART TWO

THE FIGHTING FORESTERS

- [ ] Three long legs
- [ ] Knights shooting arrows at knights
- [ ] Knights being chopped down by a tree
- [ ] Two multiple knock-outs
- [ ] Eight pairs of upside-down feet
- [ ] A tree with a lot of puff
- [ ] Hard-headed women
- [ ] Attackers about to be attacked
- [ ] A strong woman and a weak one
- [ ] An easily frightened horse
- [ ] A lazy lady
- [ ] A three-legged knight
- [ ] An upside-down ladder
- [ ] Loving trees
- [ ] An upside-down trunk
- [ ] A two-headed unicorn
- [ ] A unicorn in a tree
- [ ] Foliage faces
- [ ] Muddy mud-slingers
- [ ] A tearful small tree
- [ ] Spears getting sharpened tips
- [ ] Trees branching out violently
- [ ] Stilts being chewed up

THE DEEP-SEA DIVERS

- [ ] A two-headed fish
- [ ] A sword fight with a swordfish
- [ ] A sea bed
- [ ] A fish face
- [ ] A catfish and a dogfish
- [ ] A jellyfish
- [ ] A fish with two tails
- [ ] Two fish-shaped formations
- [ ] A sea-lion
- [ ] A skate
- [ ] Treacherous treasure
- [ ] Oyster-beds
- [ ] Tinned fish, flying fish and fish fingers
- [ ] Electric eels
- [ ] A deck of cards
- [ ] A bottle in a message
- [ ] A fake fin
- [ ] A back to front mermaid
- [ ] A seahorse-drawn carriage
- [ ] A boat's compass
- [ ] A fish fishing
- [ ] An underwater beach scene
- [ ] Divers drawing on an angry sea monster

THE KNIGHTS OF THE MAGIC FLAG

- [ ] Unfaithful royals
- [ ] A flag full of fists
- [ ] A game of noughts and crosses
- [ ] A sword-fighting reindeer
- [ ] A man behind bars
- [ ] A mouse among lions
- [ ] Flags within a flag
- [ ] A tangle of tongues
- [ ] A flag covered in axes
- [ ] A zebra crossing
- [ ] A puffing spoilsport
- [ ] A battering-ram door key
- [ ] Snakes and ladders
- [ ] A flame-throwing dragon
- [ ] Diminishing puddings
- [ ] A crown thief
- [ ] A thirsty lion
- [ ] A weapons imbalance
- [ ] A foot being tickled by a feather
- [ ] Some cheeky soldiers
- [ ] A surrendering reindeer
- [ ] A dog straining to get a bone
- [ ] A helmet with three eyes

THE UNFRIENDLY GIANTS

- [ ] Trappers about to be trapped
- [ ] A catapulted missile hitting people
- [ ] Three people in a giant hood
- [ ] Ducks out of water
- [ ] A mocking giant about to be struck
- [ ] A giant with a roof over his head
- [ ] Two giants who are out for the count
- [ ] Two windmill knock-outs
- [ ] A polite giant about to get a headache
- [ ] Two broom trees
- [ ] A hairy bird's nest
- [ ] A battering-ram fist
- [ ] A house-shaker
- [ ] People taking part in a board game
- [ ] A landslide of boulders
- [ ] A drawing-pin trap
- [ ] Six people loading two slingshots
- [ ] Six people strapped inside giant belts
- [ ] Rope-pullers being pulled
- [ ] Birds being disturbed by a giant
- [ ] Two game-watchers slapping people
- [ ] Four shy ladies being flattered
- [ ] A powerful burst of pond water

THE UNDERGROUND HUNTERS

- [ ] A hunter about to put his foot in it
- [ ] Four frightened flames
- [ ] A snaky hat thief
- [ ] An underground traffic policeman
- [ ] Three surrendering flames
- [ ] A two-headed snake
- [ ] A ridiculously long snake
- [ ] A dragon that attacks with both ends
- [ ] Three dragons wearing sunglasses
- [ ] A snaky tickle
- [ ] Angry snake-parents
- [ ] Five broken spears
- [ ] A monstrous bridge
- [ ] Five rock faces
- [ ] Upside-down hunters
- [ ] A snake that is trapped
- [ ] A very long ladder
- [ ] A torch setting fire to spears
- [ ] Hunters tripped by a tongue
- [ ] A hunter with an extra-long spear
- [ ] Hunters about to collide
- [ ] Hunters going round in a circle
- [ ] A shocked tail-puller

THE LAND OF WALLIES

- [ ] Wallies waving
- [ ] Wallies walking
- [ ] Wallies running
- [ ] Wallies sitting
- [ ] Wallies lying down
- [ ] Wallies standing still
- [ ] Wallies giving the thumbs-up
- [ ] Wallies looking frightened
- [ ] Wallies searching
- [ ] Wallies being chased
- [ ] Wallies smiling
- [ ] Wallies sliding
- [ ] Wallies with bobble hats
- [ ] Wallies without bobble hats
- [ ] Wallies raising their bobble hats
- [ ] Wallies with walking sticks
- [ ] Wallies without walking sticks
- [ ] Wallies with spectacles
- [ ] Wallies without spectacles
- [ ] A Wally on a hat
- [ ] A Wally holding a wing
- [ ] Wally

THE FANTASTIC JOURNEY

Did you find Wally, his friends and all the things that they had lost? Did you find the mystery character who appeared in every scene except the Land of Wallies? It may be difficult, but keep searching and eventually you'll find him – now that's a clue! And one last thing: somewhere one of the Wally-watchers lost the bobble from their hat. Can you find which one, and find the bobble?

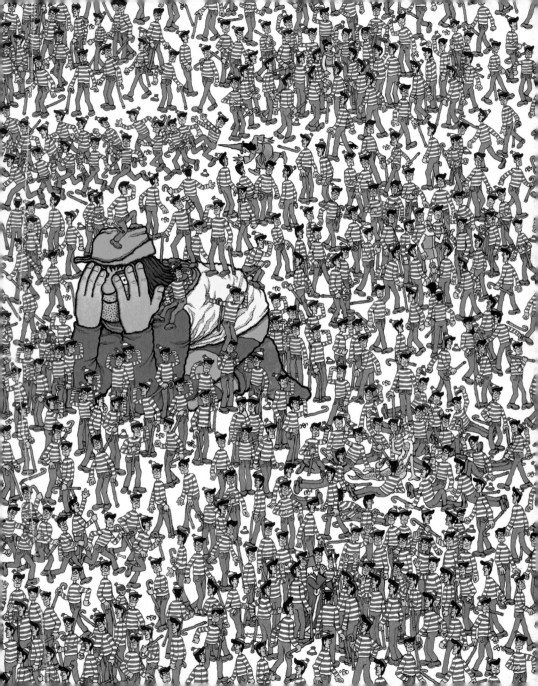

SHHH! THIS IS A SILENT MOVIE

SO THIS IS HOW THE HOLLYWOOD DREAM BEGAN – WITH SILENT MOVIES MADE IN BLACK AND WHITE. IT LOOKS CRAZY AND IT MAKES YOU LAUGH. ACTING IN SLAPSTICK COMEDIES MUST BE REALLY HARD – LOOK HOW MANY ACCIDENTS ARE HAPPENING. BUT THE GREAT THING IS THAT NONE OF THE ACTORS EVER GET HURT, HOWEVER OFTEN THEY FALL FLAT ON THEIR FACES!

FUN IN THE FOREIGN LEGION

PHEW, FILM FANS, DON'T GET OVERHEATED, THIS IS THE MOST SIZZLING LOCATION SO FAR! EVERYONE'S SWELTERING, FROM STARS TO SAND-SHIFTERS. SOME OF THOSE EXTRAS LOOK LIKE THEY'RE LOSING THEIR COOL — HAVE THEY FORGOTTEN THIS IS ONLY A FILM? PERHAPS IT'S TIME A FEW MORE OF THEM DESERTED THE DESERT AND JOINED THE RUSH FOR ICE CREAM!

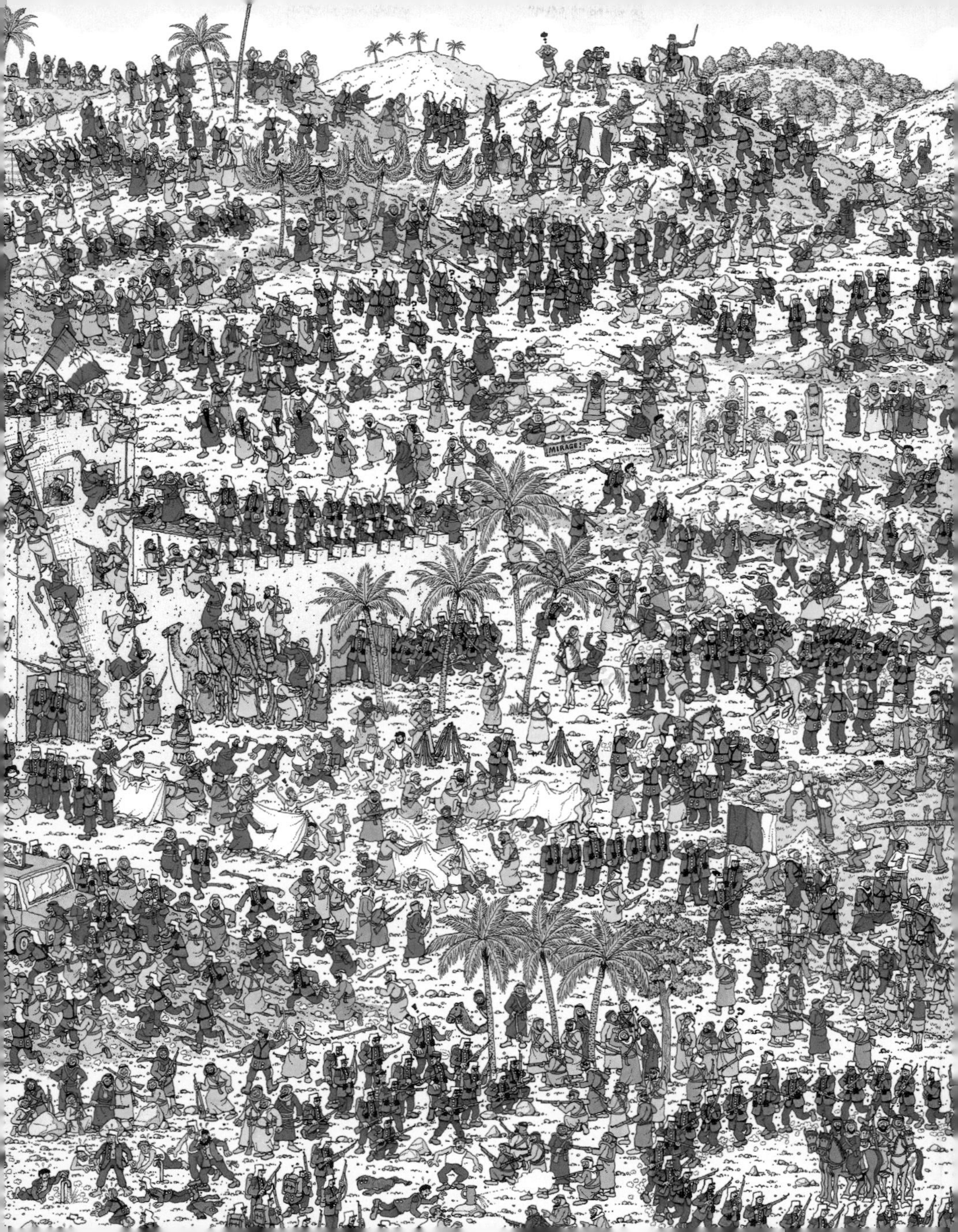
MIRAGE!

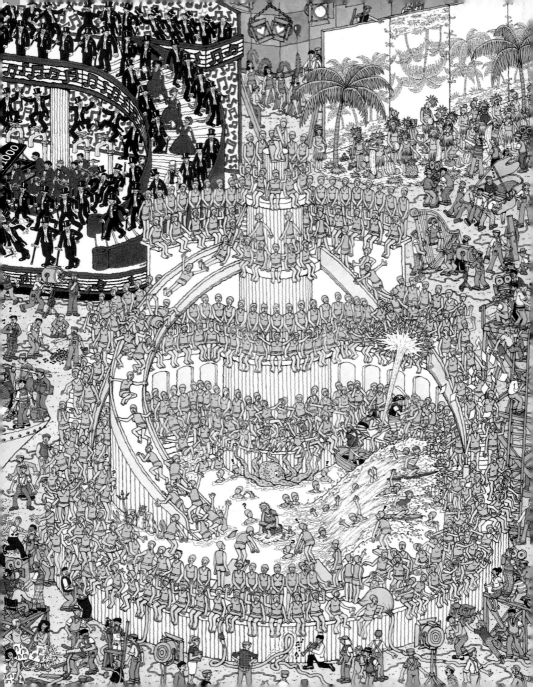

CAVE OF THE PLUNDERING PIRATES

WHAT A PLETHORA OF PLUNDERING PIRATES, WALLY-WATCHERS! WHAT A CRUSH IN THE CAVE! THERE MUST BE TONS OF TREATS AND TRINKETS IN THIS TEEMING TREASURE TROVE. WITH SPOOKY SPIRITS CENTRE STAGE AND PIRATICAL PILFERERS TO SPOT, THE DIRECTOR CERTAINLY HAS HIS HANDS FULL. LET'S HOPE HE HAS THE GOLDEN TOUCH! SHIVER-ME-TIMBERS, WHAT A FEARFULLY FUNNY FLICK THIS IS!

THE SWASHBUCKLING MUSKETEERS

ALL FOR ONE, ONE FOR ALL! – WASN'T THAT THE
MOTTO OF THE THREE MUSKETEERS? NOW LOOK
AT THIS FREE-FOR-ALL! CAN YOU SPOT OUR THREE
GALLANT HEROES BATTLING WITH THE RED-COATED
CARDINAL'S GUARDS? WITH ALL THIS SWASHBUCKLING
ACTION GOING ON, I WONDER HOW THE CAMERAMEN
CAN CAPTURE IT ALL ON FILM!

DINOSAURS, SPACEMEN AND GHOULS

PHEW, INCREDIBLE! TIME, SPACE AND HORROR ARE IN A MIGHTY MUDDLE HERE! WHAT COSMIC COSTUMES AND WHAT GREAT SPECIAL EFFECTS! ONE OF THOSE FLYING SAUCERS LOOKS LIKE IT'S REALLY FLYING! ARE THOSE REAL ALIENS INSIDE, NOT ACTORS AT ALL? SO WHAT'S REAL AND WHAT'S MADE UP IN FILMS LIKE THESE?

ROBIN HOOD'S MERRY MESS-UP

LOOK HOW MANY MERRY MEN HAVE LEFT SHERWOOD FOREST FOR A DAY OUT IN NOTTINGHAM CASTLE! AND WHAT A MERRY TIME THEY'RE HAVING, MESSING UP THE SHERIFF'S PARADE. WHICH ONE IS ROBIN HOOD? THE ONE WEARING A ROBIN HOOD, OF COURSE! WHEN YOU GO TO SEE THIS FILM, YOU'LL THINK IT'S ALL REAL, BUT THE CASTLE'S STONE WALLS ARE MADE OF WOOD!

WHEN THE STARS COME OUT

WOW, WALLY-WATCHERS, THIS IS WHAT I CALL GLAMOUR! I'M AT A MAJOR MOVIE PREMIERE. THE STARS HAVE COME TO SEE THE FILM, THE CROWDS HAVE COME TO SEE THE STARS. LOOK AT THAT PINK STRETCH LIMO – NOW THAT'S A PROPER CAR FOR A STAR. AND WHO'S IN THE BONE-MOBILE BEHIND? AND DOESN'T KING KONG LOOK NICER IN LIFE THAN WHEN HE'S ON THE SCREEN?

WHERE'S WALLY? THE MUSICAL

WOW, WHAT AN EXTRAVAGANZA, WALLY-WATCHERS – THIS ALL-SINGING, ALL-DANCING MOVIE IS ALL ABOUT ME AND MY FRIENDS! LOOK HOW MANY ACTORS ARE DRESSED UP AS ME! AND LOOK AT ALL THE WOOFS, WENDAS, WIZARD WHITEBEARDS AND ODLAWS. HAVE YOU NOTICED THAT THE WARDROBE DEPARTMENT HAS MADE MISTAKES WITH SOME OF THE ACTORS' COSTUMES? BUT THAT WON'T HELP YOU FIND THE REAL ME AND MY FOUR FRIENDS IN THIS FILM! I'LL GIVE YOU SOME CLUES. I'M THE WALLY WITH SOMETHING EXTRA FOR WOOF. ALL YOU CAN SEE OF THE REAL WOOF IS HIS TAIL. THE REAL WENDA HAS A CAMERA. THE REAL WIZARD WHITEBEARD IS WEARING A HAT BENT TO THE LEFT. AND THE REAL ODLAW IS HOLDING A WALKING STICK.
    THERE'S JUST ONE MORE THING. I'VE BEEN FOLLOWED HERE BY ONE CHARACTER FROM EVERY SET I'VE VISITED. SO CAN YOU SPOT ALL ELEVEN OF THEM IN THIS SCENE? AND CAN YOU FIND OUT WHEN EACH CHARACTER FIRST JOINED ME; AND CATCH ALL THEIR APPEARANCES THROUGHOUT MY TRAVELS?

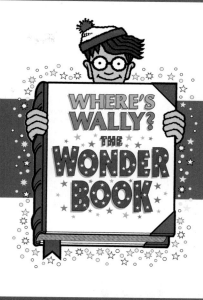

THE GREAT WHERE'S WALLY? THE WONDER BOOK CHECKLIST: PART ONE

More wonderful things for Wally fans to check out! Don't forget PART TWO at the end of this adventure!

ONCE UPON A PAGE...

- [ ] Helen of Troy and Paris
- [ ] Rudyard Kipling and the jungle book
- [ ] Sir Francis and his drake
- [ ] Wild Bill hiccup
- [ ] A shopping centaur
- [ ] Handel's water music
- [ ] George washing ton
- [ ] Samuel peeps at his diary
- [ ] Guy forks
- [ ] Tchaikovsky and the nut cracker sweet
- [ ] A roundhead with a round head
- [ ] Pythagoras and the square of the hippopotamus
- [ ] William shakes spear
- [ ] Madame two swords
- [ ] Garibaldi and his biscuits
- [ ] Florence and her nightingale
- [ ] The pilgrim fathers
- [ ] Captain cook
- [ ] Hamlet making an omelette
- [ ] Jason and the juggernauts
- [ ] Whistling Whistler painting his mother
- [ ] The Queen of Hearts
- [ ] Lincoln and the Gettysburg address
- [ ] Stephenson's rocket
- [ ] Two knights fighting the war of the roses
- [ ] The Duke of Wellington's wellington

THE MIGHTY FRUIT FIGHT

- [ ] A box of dates next to a box of dates
- [ ] A pair of date palms
- [ ] "An apple a day keeps the doctor away!"
- [ ] Six crab apples
- [ ] Four naval oranges
- [ ] Blueberries wearing blue berets
- [ ] A kiwi fruit
- [ ] A banana doing the splits
- [ ] A pine apple
- [ ] Three fruit fools
- [ ] A bowl of fruit and a can of fruit
- [ ] Cranberry saws
- [ ] An orange upsetting the apple cart
- [ ] A banana tree
- [ ] Cooking apples
- [ ] Elder berry wine
- [ ] Seven wild cherries
- [ ] Goose berries
- [ ] A pound of apples
- [ ] A partridge in a pear tree
- [ ] A fruit cock tail
- [ ] Two peach halves
- [ ] "The Big Apple"
- [ ] One sour apple without a beard
- [ ] Paw paw fruit
- [ ] Another apple cart being upset

THE GAME OF GAMES

- [ ] Some stair cases
- [ ] Maize inside a maze
- [ ] A cross word
- [ ] A flight of stairs
- [ ] A map reading
- [ ] A player rolling the dice
- [ ] A tightrope walking
- [ ] A player with a map and a pair of compasses
- [ ] A player throwing a six
- [ ] One player not wearing gloves
- [ ] One lost glove
- [ ] The other lost glove
- [ ] A missing puzzle piece
- [ ] A bad mathematician
- [ ] Eight shovels
- [ ] Twenty-nine hoops
- [ ] Two pots of paint
- [ ] An upside down question mark on a player's tunic
- [ ] A blue player holding a green block
- [ ] A player with a magnet
- [ ] Five referees with their arms folded
- [ ] Five crying players with handkerchiefs
- [ ] Two players reading newspapers
- [ ] A smoke signal
- [ ] Three ticklish players
- [ ] Eight messages in bottles

TOYS! TOYS! TOYS!

- [ ] Two spinning tops and a top spinning
- [ ] Jack-in-the-box
- [ ] A jack in a box
- [ ] A toy soldier being decorated
- [ ] A toy soldier in full dress uniform
- [ ] A toy drill sergeant
- [ ] A fish tank
- [ ] Four baby's bottles
- [ ] Two anchors
- [ ] A toy figure on skis
- [ ] A chalkboard
- [ ] A toy figure pushing a wheelbarrow
- [ ] A crow's-nest
- [ ] An apple tree bookend
- [ ] A goal
- [ ] Five big red books
- [ ] A teddy bear on a rocking horse
- [ ] A toy bandsman holding cymbals
- [ ] A toy performer balancing two chairs in the air
- [ ] Five wooden ladders
- [ ] A giraffe with a red-and-white-striped scarf
- [ ] A pirate carrying a barrel
- [ ] Toy figures climbing up a long scarf
- [ ] A teddy bear wearing a green scarf
- [ ] Two giraffes in the ark
- [ ] A robot holding a red tray

BRIGHT LIGHTS AND NIGHT FRIGHTS

- [ ] Street lights
- [ ] Lime light
- [ ] A rowing boat
- [ ] An octo-puss
- [ ] Moon light
- [ ] Light entertainers
- [ ] A very light house
- [ ] Day light
- [ ] A fishing boat
- [ ] A standard lamp
- [ ] Christmas tree lights
- [ ] A light weight boxer
- [ ] Star light
- [ ] A light at the end of the tunnel
- [ ] Stage lights
- [ ] A motor boat
- [ ] A sailor walking the plank
- [ ] A diving board
- [ ] Candle light
- [ ] A bedside light
- [ ] The deep blue C
- [ ] A Chinese lantern
- [ ] A search light
- [ ] A sleeping monster
- [ ] A mirror
- [ ] Four sailors looking through telescopes

THE CAKE FACTORY

- [ ] A loading bay
- [ ] Conveyor belts
- [ ] Two Danish pastries
- [ ] A gingerbread man
- [ ] Two workers blowing cream horns
- [ ] Maple syrup
- [ ] Hot cross buns
- [ ] A Viennese whirl
- [ ] A Swiss roll
- [ ] A pan cake
- [ ] A chocolate moose
- [ ] A custard-pie fight
- [ ] Apple pie
- [ ] Black forest gateau
- [ ] A fish cake
- [ ] Rock cakes
- [ ] Two kinds of dough nut
- [ ] A doe nut
- [ ] Baked Alaska pudding
- [ ] A fairy cake
- [ ] Mississippi mud pie
- [ ] Upside-down cake
- [ ] Carrot cake
- [ ] A cup cake
- [ ] Sponge cakes
- [ ] A cake carrying a worker

THE GREAT WHERE'S WALLY? IN HOLLYWOOD CHECKLIST: PART TWO

Even more things for
Wally-watchers
to look for.

★ THE SWASHBUCKLING MUSKETEERS ★

- [ ] Eleven gentlemen bowing
- [ ] Two wheelbarrows
- [ ] Twelve spouts of water
- [ ] A tear-jerking emotional scene
- [ ] A gentleman with only one glove
- [ ] Badly dressed men turned away from the dance
- [ ] Three musket tears
- [ ] One lost glove
- [ ] Four real animals
- [ ] A man wearing different coloured gloves
- [ ] A bouncer
- [ ] Three angry gardeners
- [ ] Two swordsmen "fencing"
- [ ] Three mixed-up statues
- [ ] A man having his foot tickled
- [ ] Four ladies being presented with flowers
- [ ] A hat with a striped plume

★ DINOSAURS, SPACEMEN AND GHOULS ★

- [ ] "Hand" luggage
- [ ] A fly in saucer
- [ ] A ticklish dinosaur
- [ ] A greedy green alien
- [ ] A dozing dinosaur
- [ ] A spaceship
- [ ] Stars in a star's dressing room
- [ ] A cheeky dinosaur
- [ ] A planet picnic
- [ ] A game of hoopla
- [ ] A wolfman having a howling good time
- [ ] Eight characters in craters
- [ ] A spacecastle
- [ ] Two people reading books
- [ ] Four cavemen going up in the world
- [ ] An astronaut without helmet, gloves or boots
- [ ] Two bottles of ketchup

★ ROBIN HOOD'S MERRY MESS-UP ★

- [ ] Eight ladies in medieval costume
- [ ] "Little" John leading some men
- [ ] A man with a bow and arrow
- [ ] Two archers with long bows
- [ ] "Maid" Marian cleaning
- [ ] A medieval extra with a radio
- [ ] A soldier with a large shield
- [ ] A night in armour
- [ ] Twenty-one ladders
- [ ] "Frier" Tuck
- [ ] Sixteen flags
- [ ] A sheriff's soldier with rolled-up sleeves
- [ ] A knight with a pink plume in his helmet
- [ ] Medieval soldiers wearing the wrong trousers
- [ ] A prisoner with a giant ball and chain
- [ ] Five real four-legged animals
- [ ] The Sheriff of Nottingham
- [ ] Seven helmets with animal crests

★★ WHEN THE STARS COME OUT ★★

- [ ] Twenty-nine lights
- [ ] Two rival news reporters
- [ ] Someone who has it all wrapped up
- [ ] A policeman wanting an autograph
- [ ] A sleepy spectator with an alarm clock
- [ ] Someone making their mark
- [ ] Six large palms
- [ ] Ten hearts
- [ ] Three cowboys
- [ ] A twisting telescope
- [ ] Someone with a bird's-eye view
- [ ] Two astronauts
- [ ] A handful of spectators
- [ ] A celebrity wearing a new dress
- [ ] An extra-long straw
- [ ] Four celebrities wearing sunglasses

★★ WHERE'S WALLY? THE MUSICAL ★★

- [ ] A Wally jumper with stripes in reverse order
- [ ] A Wally wearing a bobble hat in reverse colours
- [ ] An Odlaw wearing a hat without a bobble
- [ ] A Wenda without any shoes
- [ ] A Wally wearing shades
- [ ] An Odlaw without a moustache
- [ ] A Wally jumper with extra stripes
- [ ] A Wenda without glasses
- [ ] A Wally wearing a hat without a bobble
- [ ] A Wally without pockets on his jeans
- [ ] A Wizard Whitebeard wearing glasses
- [ ] A Wally script reading
- [ ] A sound mixer
- [ ] A haredresser
- [ ] A walking stick
- [ ] Two Wizard Whitebeards without beards
- [ ] A Wally without glasses
- [ ] A Wally with a beard
- [ ] A Wenda with blonde hair
- [ ] A Wally with blond hair
- [ ] A Wenda with a blue-and-white-striped umbrella
- [ ] A Wizard Whitebeard wearing a red hat
- [ ] A Woof wearing a bobble hat in reverse colours
- [ ] A Wenda wearing round Wally glasses
- [ ] A Wally tickling another Wally
- [ ] A Woof without a bobble hat
- [ ] A Wenda with no pockets on her skirt
- [ ] A Wally holding a walking stick the wrong way up
- [ ] A Woof wearing a hat without a bobble
- [ ] A Woof wearing shades
- [ ] A back view of a Wenda
- [ ] A Wally in blue-and-white stripes
- [ ] A Wenda who is not wearing a bobble hat
- [ ] An Odlaw without shades
- [ ] A Wizard Whitebeard dancing
- [ ] A back view of a Wally
- [ ] A Wizard Whitebeard wearing a bobble hat
- [ ] A Woof wearing a blue-and-white bobble hat
- [ ] Two Wizard Whitebeards with brown beards
- [ ] A Wenda wearing a hat without a bobble
- [ ] A Wally with two bobble hats

★★★ BACK TO THE BEGINNING ★★★

Did you find Wally, all his friends and all the things they lost? Did you find the mystery character who appears in every scene except the last? And one more thing: somewhere in the book, one of the Wally-watchers lost the bobble from his hat. Can you spot which one and find the bobble?

★★★ THE FINAL FILM TEST ★★★

Nearly all the faces in the sprocket holes on this and on PART ONE of the checklist appear in colour somewhere else in the book. Can you find where? But . . . ten of them do *not* appear anywhere else! Can you tell which ten? Lastly . . . some faces appear more than once in the sprocket holes. Can you see which ones, and how many times each one appears?

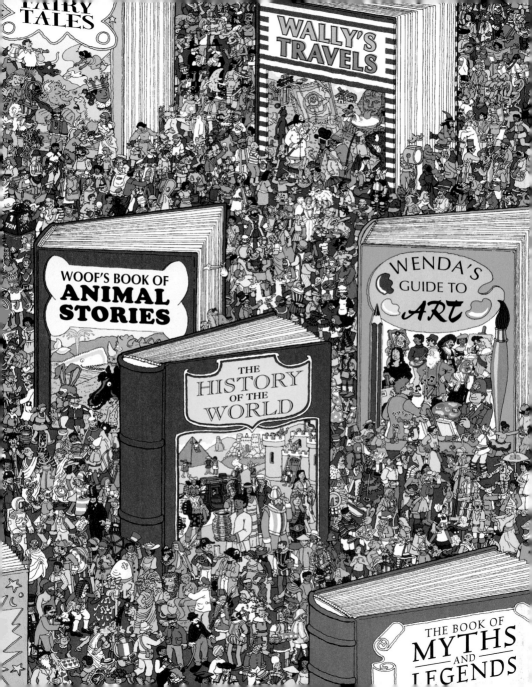

THE GAME OF GAMES

FOUR HUGE TEAMS ARE PLAYING THIS GREAT GAME OF GAMES. THE REFEREES ARE TRYING TO SEE THAT NO ONE BREAKS THE RULES. BETWEEN THE STARTING-LINE AT THE TOP AND THE FINISHING-LINE AT THE BOTTOM, THERE ARE LOTS OF PUZZLES, BOOBY-TRAPS AND TESTS. THE GREEN TEAM'S NEARLY WON, AND THE ORANGE TEAM'S HARDLY STARTED! CAN YOU SPOT THE ONLY ORANGE TEAM PLAYER WHO HAS FINISHED? AND THE ONLY GREEN TEAM PLAYER WHO HAS NOT YET BEGUN?

THE CAKE FACTORY

Mmmm! FEAST YOUR EYES, WALLY-WATCHERS! SNIFF THE DELICIOUS SMELLS OF BAKING CAKES! DROOL AT THE TASTY TOPPINGS! CAN YOU SEE A CAKE LIKE A TEAPOT, A CAKE LIKE A HOUSE, A CAKE SO TALL A WORKER ON THE FLOOR ABOVE IS LICKING IT? CAKES, CAKES, EVERYWHERE! HOW SCRUMP-TIOUS! HOW YUM-YUM-YUMPTIOUS!

LOOK AT THE OOZING SUGAR ICING AND THE SHINY RED CHERRIES ON THE ROOF UP THERE! THAT ROOM IS WHERE THE FACTORY CONTROLLERS WORK, BUT HAVE THEY LOST CONTROL?

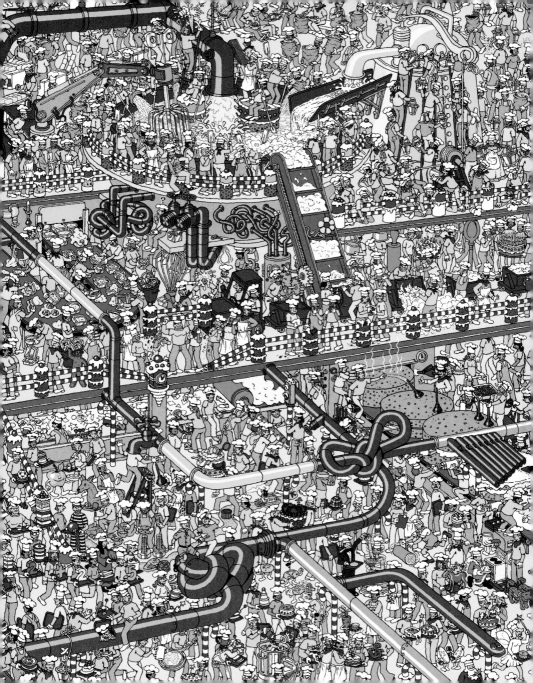

THE ODLAW SWAMP

THE BRAVE ARMY OF MANY HATS IS TRYING TO GET THROUGH THIS FEARFUL SWAMP. HUNDREDS OF ODLAWS AND BLACK-AND-YELLOW SWAMP CREATURES ARE CAUSING TROUBLE IN THE UNDERGROWTH. THE REAL ODLAW IS THE ONE CLOSEST TO HIS LOST PAIR OF BINOCULARS. CAN YOU FIND HIM, X-RAY-EYED ONES? HOW MANY DIFFERENT KINDS OF HAT CAN YOU SEE ON THE SOLDIERS' HEADS? SQUELCH! SQUELCH! I'M GLAD I'M NOT IN THEIR SHOES! ESPECIALLY AS THEIR FEET ARE IN THE MURKY MUD!

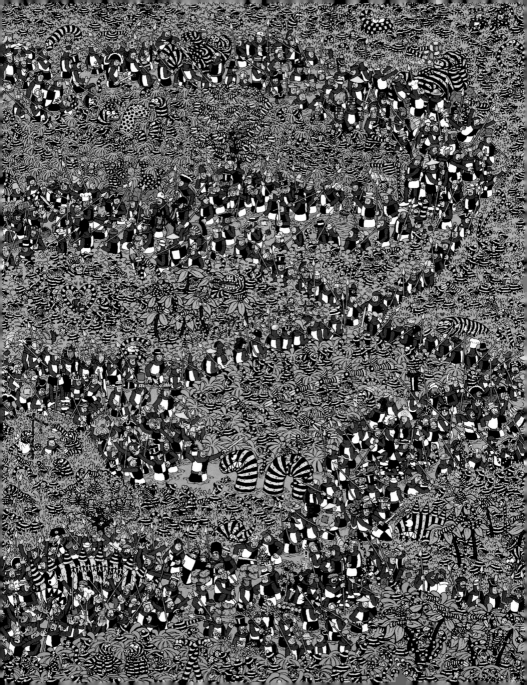

CLOWN TOWN

CLAP YOUR FEET, WALLY JOKERS! STAMP YOUR HANDS! YOU'LL GO OOGLY-BOOGLY-WOOGLY-EYED WITH WONDER! HERE ARE HUNDREDS OF CLOWNS PLAYING PRANKS AND MAKING MISCHIEF! LOOK AT THEIR COLOURFUL COSTUMES – WITH FLUFFY POMPOMS GALORE! AND THEIR BRIGHT AND SHINY NOSES! TOOT, TOOT! CAN YOU SEE A CAR WITH ITS TONGUE STICKING OUT?

TING-A-LING! AND A BIKE WITH SQUARE WHEELS? TEE, HEE! HA, HA! WHAT HAPPINESS IT IS TO BE IN CLOWN TOWN! SPLASH! SPLAT! EXCEPT FOR ALL THOSE SQUIRTY FLOWERS AND CUSTARD PIES!

THE FANTASTIC FLOWER GARDEN

WOW! WHAT A BRIGHT AND DAZZLING GARDEN SPECTACLE! ALL THE FLOWERS ARE IN FULL BLOOM, AND HUNDREDS OF BUSY GARDENERS ARE WATERING AND TENDING THEM. THE PETAL COSTUMES THEY ARE WEARING MAKE THEM LOOK LIKE FLOWERS THEMSELVES! VEGETABLES ARE GROWING IN THE GARDEN TOO. HOW MANY DIFFERENT KINDS

CAN YOU SEE? SNIFF THE AIR, WALLY FOLLOWERS! SMELL THE FANTASTIC SCENTS! WHAT A TREAT FOR YOUR NOSES AS WELL AS YOUR EYES!

THE CORRIDORS OF TIME

TICK-TOCK, TICK-TOCK! THE HANDS OF ALL THE CLOCKS EXCEPT ONE SAY A QUARTER TO TWELVE. WHAT A DING-DONG THERE WILL BE WHEN THEY STRIKE! CAN YOU FIND THE ONLY CLOCK THAT TELLS A DIFFERENT TIME? IN THIS SCENE ARE THIRTY-SEVEN DOORS. ABOVE EACH DOOR APPEARS THE SHAPE OF THE KEY THAT WILL UNLOCK IT. CAN YOU FIND THE KEYS IN THE CROWD, BRAINY ONES, AND MATCH THEM TO THE SHAPES? OH NO! ONE DOOR HAS NO SHAPE ABOVE IT! EVEN SO YOU MUST FIND ITS KEY!

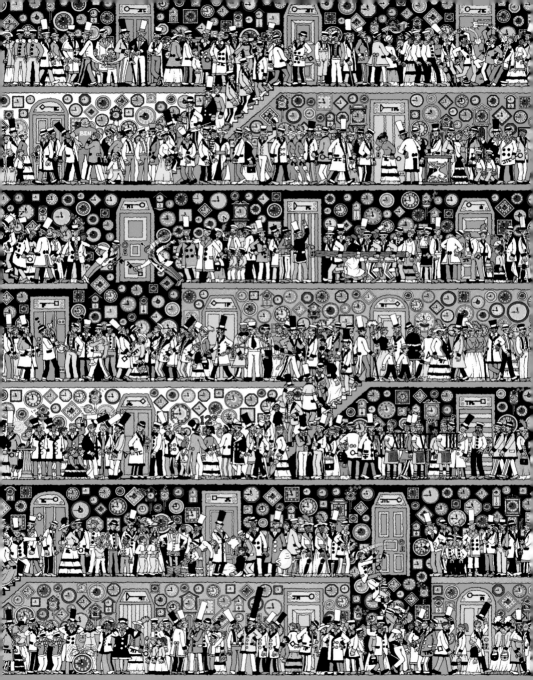

THE LAND OF WOOFS

HEY! LOOK AT ALL THESE DOGS THAT ARE DRESSED LIKE WOOF! BOW, WOW, WOW! IN THIS LAND, A DOG'S LIFE IS THE HIGH LIFE! THERE'S A LUXURY WOOF HOTEL WITH A BONE-SHAPED SWIMMING POOL, AND AT THE WOOF RACETRACK LOTS OF WOOFS ARE CHASING ATTENDANTS DRESSED AS CATS, SAUSAGES AND POSTMEN! THE BOOKMARK IS ON THIS PAGE, WALLY FOLLOWERS, SO NOW YOU KNOW, THIS IS MY FAVOURITE SCENE! THIS IS THE ONLY SCENE IN THE BOOK WHERE YOU CAN SEE MORE OF THE REAL WOOF THAN JUST HIS TAIL! BUT CAN YOU FIND HIM? HE'S THE ONLY ONE WITH FIVE RED STRIPES ON HIS TAIL! HERE'S ANOTHER CHALLENGE! ELEVEN

TRAVELLERS HAVE FOLLOWED ME HERE – ONE FROM EVERY SCENE. CAN YOU SEE THEM? AND CAN YOU FIND WHERE EACH ONE JOINED ME ON MY ADVENTURES, AND SPOT ALL THEIR APPEARANCES AFTERWARDS? KEEP ON SEARCHING, WALLY FANS! HAVE A WONDERFUL, WONDERFUL TIME!

THE GREAT WHERE'S WALLY?
THE WONDER BOOK CHECKLIST: PART TWO

THE BATTLE OF THE BANDS

- A rubber band
- A piano forty
- A pipe band
- Bandsmen "playing" their instruments
- A fan fair
- Bandsmen with saxophones and sacks of phones
- A steel band
- A swing band
- Sheet music
- Racing bandsmen "beating" their drums
- A rock band
- Kettle drums
- A mouth organ
- A baby sitar
- A 1-man band
- A French horn
- A barrel organ
- Some violin bows
- A rock and roll band
- Bandsmen playing cornets
- A drummer with drumsticks
- A big elephant trunk
- Bandsmen making a drum kit
- The orchestra pit
- A bag piper
- Some cheetah bandsmen cheating

THE ODLAW SWAMP

- Two soldiers disguised as Odlaws
- A soldier wearing a bowler hat
- A soldier wearing a stovepipe hat
- A soldier wearing a riding helmet
- A soldier wearing a straw hat
- Three soldiers wearing peaked caps
- A lady wearing an Easter bonnet
- Two soldiers wearing American football helmets
- Two soldiers wearing baseball caps
- A big shield next to a little shield
- A lady wearing a sun hat
- A soldier with two big feathers in his hat
- Some rattle snakes
- Five romantic snakes
- Seven wooden rafts
- Three small wooden boats
- Four birds' nests
- One Odlaw in disguise
- A swamp creature without stripes
- A monster cleaning its teeth
- A monster asleep, but not for long
- A soldier floating on a parcel
- A very big monster with a very small head
- One charmed snake
- Five charmed spears
- A snake reading

CLOWN TOWN

- A clown reading a newspaper
- A starry umbrella
- A clown with a blue teapot
- Two hoses leaking
- A clown with two hoops on each arm
- A clown looking through a telescope
- Two clowns holding big hammers
- A clown with a bag of crackers
- Two clowns holding flowerpots
- A clown swinging a pillow
- A clown combing the roof of a Clown Town house
- A clown bursting a balloon
- Six flowers squirting the same clown
- A clown wearing a Jack-in-the-box hat
- Three cars
- Three watering-cans
- A clown with a fishing rod
- One hat joining two clowns
- A clown about to catapult a custard pie
- Clowns wearing tea shirts
- Three clowns with buckets of water
- A clown with a yo-yo
- A clown stepping into a custard pie
- Seventeen clouds
- A clown having his foot tickled
- One clown with a green nose

THE FANTASTIC FLOWER GARDEN

- The yellow rose of Texas
- Flower pots and flower beds
- Butter flies
- Gardeners sewing seeds and planting bulbs
- A garden nursery
- A bird bath and a bird table
- House plants, wall flowers and blue bells
- Dandy lions, tiger lilies and fox gloves
- Cabbage patches, letters leaves and a collie flower
- A hedgehog next to a hedge hog
- A flower border and a flower show
- A bull frog
- Earth worms
- A wheelbarrow full of wheels
- A cricket match
- Parsley, sage, Rosemary and time
- A queen bee near a honey comb
- A landscape gardener
- A sun dial next to a sundial
- Gardeners dancing to the beetles
- A green house and a tree house
- A spring onion and a leek with a leak
- Door mice
- An apple tree
- Weeping willows and climbing roses
- Rock pool

THE CORRIDORS OF TIME

- The clock striking twelve
- An egg timer
- Wall clocks, clock faces and a clock tower
- A very loud alarm clock
- A travelling clock
- A runner racing against time
- Roman numerals
- Time flies
- An hour glass
- Big Ben
- Old Father Time
- Grandfather clocks
- A walking stick
- Thirty-six pairs of almost identical twins
- One pair of identical twins
- A man's braces being pulled in opposite directions
- A swinging pendulum
- Coat tails tied in a knot
- A door and thirteen clocks on their sides
- A very tall top hat
- A sundial
- A pair of hooked umbrellas
- A clock cuckoo
- A pair of tangled walking-sticks

THE LAND OF WOOFS

- Dog biscuits
- A mountain dog
- A hot dog getting cool
- A grey hound bus
- Dog baskets
- A pair of swimming trunks
- A sheep dog
- A watch dog
- A bull dog
- A great Dane
- A guard dog
- A dog in a wet suit
- Some swimming costumes
- A dog with a red collar
- A dog wearing a yellow collar with a blue tag
- A dog with a blue bobble on his hat
- A top dog
- A sausage dog with sausages
- A dog wearing a blue collar with a green tag
- A cat dressed like a Woof dog
- The puppies' pool
- A Woof doing a paw stand
- A Scottie dog
- Two dogs having a massage
- A sniffer dog
- Twenty-two red-and-white-striped towels

★ CLOWNING AROUND! ★

Ha, ha! What a joker! The clown who follows Wally and his friends to the end of the book changes the colour of his hatband in one scene! Can you find which scene it is? What colour does his hatband change to?

THE GREAT PICTURE HUNT!

HEY, WALLY FANS, WELCOME TO THE GREAT PICTURE HUNT!

THE FUN STARTS IN EXHIBIT 1, ODLAW'S PICTURE PANDEMONIUM, WHERE YOU'LL FIND 30 ENORMOUS PORTRAITS. WOW! EXAMINE THEM CAREFULLY, BECAUSE EVERY ONE OF THE PORTRAIT SUBJECTS CAN BE FOUND SOMEWHERE ELSE IN THIS BOOK ... BUT ONLY ONCE. YOUR CHALLENGE IS TO FIND THESE SLIPPERY SUBJECTS WHEREVER THEY MIGHT BE HIDING.

ARE YOU READY FOR AN ART ADVENTURE GALLERY GAZERS? HAVE FUN!

Wally

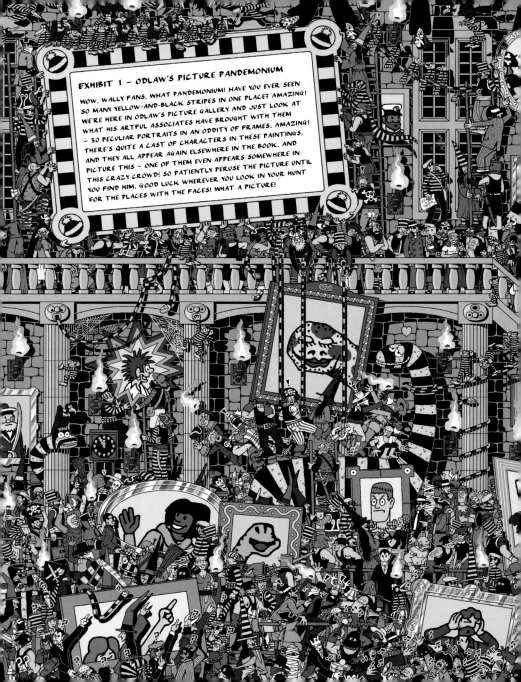

EXHIBIT 1 – ODLAW'S PICTURE PANDEMONIUM

WOW, WALLY FANS, WHAT PANDEMONIUM! HAVE YOU EVER SEEN SO MANY YELLOW-AND-BLACK STRIPES IN ONE PLACE? AMAZING! WE'RE HERE IN ODLAW'S PICTURE GALLERY AND JUST LOOK AT WHAT HIS ARTFUL ASSOCIATES HAVE BROUGHT WITH THEM – 30 PECULIAR PORTRAITS IN AN ODDITY OF FRAMES. AMAZING! THERE'S QUITE A CAST OF CHARACTERS IN THESE PAINTINGS, AND THEY ALL APPEAR AGAIN ELSEWHERE IN THE BOOK. AND PICTURE THIS – ONE OF THEM EVEN APPEARS SOMEWHERE IN THIS CRAZY CROWD! SO PATIENTLY PERUSE THE PICTURE UNTIL YOU FIND HIM. GOOD LUCK WHEREVER YOU LOOK IN YOUR HUNT FOR THE PLACES WITH THE FACES! WHAT A PICTURE!

THE SUPER WHERE'S WALLY? THE GREAT PICTURE HUNT CHECKLIST: PART ONE

Hundreds more things for gallery gazers to look for! Don't forget PART TWO at the end of this adventure!

EXHIBIT 1 – ODLAW'S PICTURE PANDEMONIUM

- [ ] A green-skinned pirate
- [ ] Two ghost imposters
- [ ] Five mummies
- [ ] A bandaged finger
- [ ] Two spiders
- [ ] A head and crossbones
- [ ] A drooping flower
- [ ] Two teddy tattoos
- [ ] A black cat
- [ ] The sun
- [ ] Eight stripy witches' hats
- [ ] Fourteen ladders
- [ ] Twelve vultures
- [ ] Upside-down skull and crossbones
- [ ] Four flying witches
- [ ] A pair of heart-shaped sunglasses
- [ ] Three spike-topped helmets
- [ ] A puzzled, fangless vampire
- [ ] A drinking straw
- [ ] A squashed Viking

EXHIBIT 2 – A SPORTING LIFE

- [ ] Hitting a hole-in-one
- [ ] A centaur circle
- [ ] A volleyball court
- [ ] Serving an Ace
- [ ] A boxer saved by the belle
- [ ] Four under Pa
- [ ] The baseball batter's swing
- [ ] A pool table
- [ ] A Jim instructor
- [ ] Dancers at a soccer ball
- [ ] Team subs
- [ ] A marshal arts class
- [ ] Weightlifters pumping iron
- [ ] Shadow boxers
- [ ] A football quarterback
- [ ] Snow-peaked caps
- [ ] A pair of swimming trunks
- [ ] An archer with a long bow
- [ ] A steeple chase
- [ ] Pear skating

SPOT THE DIFFERENCE EXHIBIT 4 – BROWN SAILORS & GREEN SCALERS AGAIN DID YOU SPOT THESE?

- [ ] A missing tail-end
- [ ] An absent cloud
- [ ] A brown balloon
- [ ] A balloon number missing
- [ ] A missing tooth
- [ ] A missing lasso
- [ ] Some missing smoke
- [ ] A missing flag
- [ ] A monster without spots
- [ ] A back-to-front number
- [ ] A missing flag number
- [ ] A missing monster
- [ ] An absent sailor
- [ ] A missing telescope
- [ ] A man with a yellow beard
- [ ] Some missing green slime
- [ ] An extra sailor
- [ ] A slime gun without a nozzle
- [ ] A brown sea-creature
- [ ] A sailor in a white top

EXHIBIT 5 – THE PINK PARADISE PARTY

- [ ] Two skate on skates
- [ ] Drainpipe trousers
- [ ] A heavy-metal guitarist
- [ ] Two mixing desks
- [ ] A pencil skirt
- [ ] Ball room dancers
- [ ] Two bugs jitterbugging
- [ ] A sole singer
- [ ] Oxford bags
- [ ] A Mini skirt
- [ ] A tea shirt
- [ ] Two fox trotters
- [ ] Platform shoes
- [ ] Some disc jockeys
- [ ] Oliver Twisting
- [ ] A Duke box and jukebox
- [ ] Dancing the knight away
- [ ] Beehive hairdos
- [ ] Squares square-dancing
- [ ] Two door men

EXHIBIT 6 – OLD FRIENDS

- [ ] A lady in a blue ball gown
- [ ] A snowman
- [ ] A monster in a man-suit
- [ ] A red astronaut
- [ ] A woman with a green bag
- [ ] A pirate surfing
- [ ] A thirsty boy
- [ ] A cook with a dough nut
- [ ] A crab clipping a toenail
- [ ] A hippo with a jumbo-sized toothbrush
- [ ] A pole vaulter taking a break
- [ ] A rude statue
- [ ] A bull frog
- [ ] A man holding a flower
- [ ] A man in a manhole
- [ ] A horse-drawn wagon
- [ ] A woman with a clipboard
- [ ] A swimmer in shades
- [ ] A dog in the shade
- [ ] A woman holding a hairbrush

EXHIBIT 1 – ODLAW'S PICTURE PANDEMONIUM

WOW, WALLY FANS, WHAT PANDEMONIUM! HAVE YOU EVER SEEN SO MANY YELLOW-AND-BLACK STRIPES IN ONE PLACE? AMAZING! WE'RE HERE IN ODLAW'S PICTURE GALLERY AND JUST LOOK AT WHAT HIS ARTFUL ASSOCIATES HAVE BROUGHT WITH THEM – 30 PECULIAR PORTRAITS IN AN ODDITY OF FRAMES. AMAZING! THERE'S QUITE A CAST OF CHARACTERS IN THESE PAINTINGS, AND THEY ALL APPEAR AGAIN ELSEWHERE IN THE BOOK. AND PICTURE THIS – ONE OF THEM EVEN APPEARS SOMEWHERE IN THIS CRAZY CROWD! SO PATIENTLY PERUSE THE PICTURE UNTIL YOU FIND HIM. GOOD LUCK WHEREVER YOU LOOK IN YOUR HUNT FOR THE PLACES WITH THE FACES! WHAT A PICTURE!

EXHIBIT 2 –
A SPORTING LIFE

WELCOME, PICTURE HUNT PALS, TO MY SPECIAL REPORT FROM THE LAND OF SPORT. FANTASTIC! IT'S LIKE THE OLYMPICS EVERY DAY HERE, BUT WITH SO MANY ATHLETIC EVENTS ON THE MENU THERE'S NO TIME LEFT FOR ANY REST AND RELAXATION. HOWEVER, THERE'S NOTHING TOO STRENUOUS ABOUT OUR MAIN EVENT, THE GREAT PICTURE HUNT, SO KEEP YOUR EYES ON THE BALL AND HAVE YOUR POINTER FINGERS READY. ON YOUR MARKS, GET SET, GO!

EXHIBIT 4 –
BROWN SAILORS &
GREEN SCALERS AGAIN
WHAT BAL-LOON-ERY IS THIS,
WALLY FANS? THE SAME PICTURE AGAIN? NOT
QUITE THE SAME, BUT AN ALMOST PERFECT
COPY. WOW! AMAZING! CAN YOU SPOT
ALL 20 DIFFERENCES?

EXHIBIT 5 – THE PINK PARADISE PARTY

IT'S SATURDAY NIGHT, THE TEMPERATURE IS RISING AND IT LOOKS AS IF A RASH OF MUSICAL MAYHEM AND DISCO FEVER HAS BROKEN OUT IN THIS DIZZY DANCE HALL. WOW! AMAZING! HIP HIP-HOPPERS, BODY-POPPERS, ROCK-AND-ROLLERS AND BODY-AND-SOULERS – IT'S A PACKED-OUT, PARTYGOERS' PINK PARADISE. SO GET ON DOWN, CUT YOUR GROOVE AND MAKE YOUR MOVES – IT'S TIME TO SHUFFLE YOUR FEET TO THE PICTURE HUNT BEAT!

EXHIBIT 7 – OLD FRIENDS AGAIN

IT'S ALWAYS NICE WHEN FRIENDS CAN STAY FOR A LITTLE LONGER ... I'VE CALLED THIS "OLD FRIENDS AGAIN" BECAUSE THAT'S EXACTLY WHAT IT IS ... A FRAMED COLLECTION OF SOME OF THE OLD FRIENDS FROM THE PICTURE NEXT DOOR, BUT IN SILHOUETTE FORM. AND JUST TO MAKE IT A BIT MORE INTERESTING, SOME OF THEM ARE PICTURED UPSIDE DOWN OR SIDEWAYS. CAN YOU MATCH EACH SILHOUETTE HERE WITH THE CORRECT OLD FRIEND IN EXHIBIT 6? SO, ONWARDS AND UPWARDS (AND DOWNWARDS AND SIDEWAYS), MY PICTURE HUNT PORTRAITEERS!

EXHIBIT 8 – THE MONSTER MASTERPIECE

YIKES, SPIKES AND KNOBBLY BITS, I'M LOST IN THE LAND OF THE MONSTERS. WOW! WHAT A CREATURE FEATURE! WHO'S IN CHARGE HERE, ANYWAY? THE HELMETED HUNTERS OR THEIR QUARRELSOME QUARRY? BUT DON'T BE PUT OFF BY THIS MONSTER MAYHEM, ART FANS, PLAY ON WITH THE PUZZLE, THERE ARE STILL SOME PORTRAIT SUBJECTS TO FIND. WHAT A MONSTROSITY!

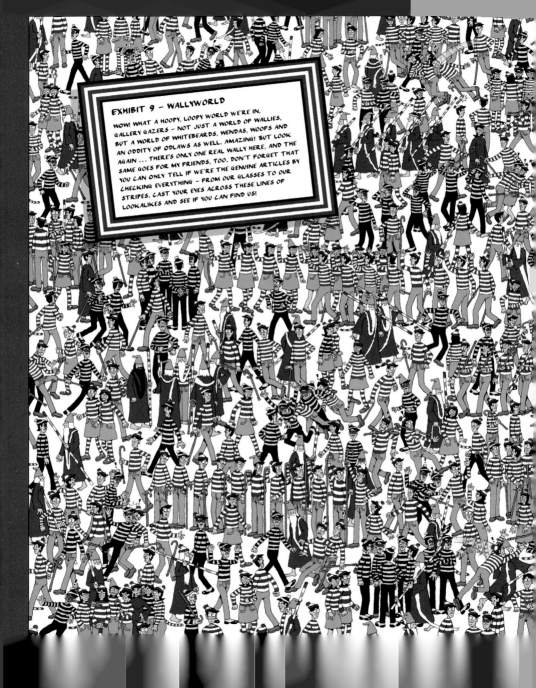

EXHIBIT 9 – WALLYWORLD

WOW! WHAT A HOOPY, LOOPY WORLD WE'RE IN,
GALLERY GAZERS – NOT JUST A WORLD OF WALLIES,
BUT A WORLD OF WHITEBEARDS, WENDAS, WOOFS AND
AN ODDITY OF ODLAWS AS WELL. AMAZING! BUT LOOK
AGAIN ... THERE'S ONLY ONE REAL WALLY HERE, AND THE
SAME GOES FOR MY FRIENDS, TOO. DON'T FORGET THAT
YOU CAN ONLY TELL IF WE'RE THE GENUINE ARTICLES BY
CHECKING EVERYTHING – FROM OUR GLASSES TO OUR
STRIPES. CAST YOUR EYES ACROSS THESE LINES OF
LOOKALIKES AND SEE IF YOU CAN FIND US!

EXHIBIT 10 – WALLYWORLD AGAIN

DON'T BE DAUNTED BY HAVING TO DALLY OVER THIS
DIZZY DIORAMA OF DOPPELGANGERS, DEAR READERS,
EVERYTHING IS NOT AS IT LOOKS. WE'RE ALL STILL
HERE, BUT THIS TIME THERE ARE 20 VARIATIONS FROM
THE SCENE ON THE LEFT. CAN YOU SPOT ALL THE
DIFFERENCES? AND HAVE YOU FOUND THE REAL ME AND
THE REAL WHITEBEARD, WENDA, WOOF AND ODLAW YET?
IF YOU'RE STILL HAVING TROUBLE FINDING US, WHY NOT
CHECK OUT HOW WE LOOK ON THE FIRST PAGE.

EXHIBIT 11 – PIRATE PANORAMA

SHIVER ME TIMBERS, SHIPMATES, WHAT PERFIDIOUS, PIRATE PANORAMA IS THIS? WOW! AMAZING! I'VE SAILED THE SEVEN SEAS SEARCHING FOR THESE 30 PORTRAIT PEOPLE, AND NOW THAT OUR JOURNEY IS ALMOST OVER, I JUST HOPE THE PIRATES DON'T MAKE THEM WALK THE PLANK! I'M SURE THOSE FARAWAY CASTAWAYS WOULD PREFER TO BE MAROONED ON A DESERT ISLAND THAN TO MEET THESE BARMY BUCCANEERS. ALL HANDS ON DECK!

EXHIBIT 12 – THE GREAT PORTRAIT EXHIBITION

OUR JOURNEY IS NOW OVER, PORTRAIT PERUSERS, BUT WHAT A FITTING FINALE: A FANTASTIC EXHIBITION IN A PROPER ART GALLERY. WOW! AMAZING! THE CROWD HERE SEEMS MUCH MORE WELCOMING THAN ODLAW'S ODD ENSEMBLE. I'M ALSO REALLY PLEASED THAT ALL 30 OF THE CHARACTERS WE'VE BEEN HUNTING FOR ARE HERE AMONGST THE GALLERY GAZERS. SEE IF YOU CAN SPOT THEM AS THEY WANDER FREELY AMONGST THE VISITORS ENJOYING THE SHOW. I HOPE YOU FOUND THEM IN THE PREVIOUS PAGES, TOO. IF NOT, THERE'S STILL PLENTY OF TIME TO DO SO – THE EXHIBITION NEVER CLOSES. HAPPY HUNTING!

THE SUPER WHERE'S WALLY?
THE GREAT PICTURE HUNT CHECKLIST: PART TWO

SPOT THE DIFFERENCE
EXHIBIT 10 – WALLYWORLD AGAIN
DID YOU SPOT THESE?

- A missing wizard
- A Wally no longer smiling
- A missing Woof's tail
- An Odlaw missing a hat
- An Odlaw wearing different glasses
- A Wenda in blue-and-white tights
- A walking stick missing a tip
- An Odlaw in yellow trousers
- A Wenda with vertical stripes
- A wizard beard that has changed colour
- A Wenda wearing a red skirt
- A Whitebeard wearing a red hat
- A Wally whose stripes have shifted
- A Whitebeard whose staff is missing
- A hat that has lost its bobble
- A Wally in stripy trousers
- A Wenda who has lost her glasses
- A Woof with a longer tail
- A missing walking stick
- A spotty Odlaw

EXHIBIT 8 – THE MONSTER MASTERPIECE

- Salt and pepper pots
- A ropey snake bite
- A monster wearing a napkin
- A tail lassoing a foot
- Two hunters using hankies
- A raft made from snakes
- A ticklish monster
- A snake tripping up hunters
- A pointed helmet prodding a hunter
- A monster munching timber
- One round shield
- Six arrows rebounding off monsters
- A swimming race
- A bunch of flowers
- A log stuck on a horn
- A monster wielding three swords
- A hunter held upside down
- A long tongue lassoing a leg
- A monster chewing spears
- Two hunter boys sliding

EXHIBIT 11 – PIRATE PANORAMA

- Seven bottles
- Diving boards
- A massage in a bottle
- A giant wave
- A school of whales
- A pirate riding the serf
- Five birds
- A deck of cards
- Seven flags
- A pirate walking the plank
- A dessert island
- Eleven cannons
- The deep blue C
- Eight fins
- A pirate with an axe and a cutlass
- A tap
- Lobster beds
- Four cannonballs
- A two-foot gun barrel
- Two coloured patches

EXHIBIT 12 – THE GREAT PORTRAIT EXHIBITION

- Nineteen flowers
- A woman guitarist
- A leaking-water colour
- Two duelling artists
- Eleven horses
- Four brooms
- An empty red frame
- Two cavewomen
- A very long white beard
- Nine fish
- An artist with seven brushes
- A grey donkey
- A rude shield
- Two brushes in a hatband
- A hungry wolf
- A red bow tie
- An artist with a big brush
- Five stools
- Stripy red-and-yellow sleeves
- A cracked vase

AND JUST ONE MORE THING …

Why not brush up on your maths with this sum?

Add the number of frames containing pictures of men in Exhibit 1 to the number of blue picture frames in Exhibit 7.

Then subtract the number of triangular frames in Exhibit 12.

HI WALLY-WATCHERS!

ARE YOU READY TO JOIN ME ON ANOTHER
INCREDIBLE ADVENTURE WITH MORE FUN
AND GAMES THAN EVER BEFORE?
I SEE SO MANY WONDERFUL THINGS ON MY
TRAVELS THAT THIS TIME I AM TAKING
MY NOTEPAD TO HELP ME REMEMBER THEM.
WOW! THE EXCITEMENT BEGINS RIGHT HERE
– AS THE RED KNIGHTS STORM THE BLUE
KNIGHTS' CASTLE WALLS. CAN YOU SPOT
SOME GRINNING GARGOYLES, A GHASTLY
GHOUL AND A GIANT CAKE?

THE SEARCH IS ON!

Wally

FIND WALLY, WOOF (BUT ALL YOU CAN SEE IS HIS TAIL), WENDA,
WIZARD WHITEBEARD AND ODLAW IN EVERY SCENE. (DON'T BE
FOOLED BY ANY CHILDREN THAT ARE DRESSED LIKE WALLY!)

FIND THE PRECIOUS THINGS THEY'VE LOST TOO:
WALLY'S KEY, WOOF'S BONE, WENDA'S CAMERA, WIZARD
WHITEBEARD'S SCROLL AND ODLAW'S BINOCULARS.

ONE MORE THING! CAN YOU FIND A PIECE OF PAPER THAT
WALLY HAS DROPPED FROM HIS NOTEPAD IN EVERY SCENE?

THE GREAT WHERE'S WALLY? THE INCREDIBLE PAPER CHASE CHECKLIST: PART ONE

Hundreds more spectacular things to search for! Don't forget PART TWO at the end of this adventure!

THE CASTLE SIEGE

- [ ] Five blue-coated soldiers wearing blue plumes
- [ ] Five red-coated soldiers wearing red plumes
- [ ] A blue-coated soldier wearing a red plume
- [ ] A red-coated soldier wearing a blue plume
- [ ] Four blue-coated archers
- [ ] Five characters holding white feathers
- [ ] Some pike men holding pikes
- [ ] Minors digging a tunnel
- [ ] Twenty-two ladders
- [ ] Some longbowmen wearing long bows
- [ ] Eight catapults
- [ ] Twenty-seven ladies dressed in blue
- [ ] Twelve men with white beards
- [ ] A wishing well
- [ ] Two tidy witches
- [ ] Nine blue shields
- [ ] Four horses
- [ ] Three round red shields
- [ ] A prisoner in a puzzling position
- [ ] Eight men snoozing
- [ ] Someone with by far the longest hair
- [ ] A soldier with one bare foot
- [ ] Eighteen characters with their tongues out
- [ ] Five tents

THE JURASSIC GAMES

- [ ] A dinosaur volleyball game
- [ ] A dinosaur rowing race
- [ ] Dinosaurs playing cricket
- [ ] A dinosaur football match
- [ ] A dinosaur windsurfer race
- [ ] Dinosaurs playing baseball
- [ ] A dinosaur American football game
- [ ] Dinosaurs playing basketball
- [ ] Dinosaurs playing golf
- [ ] A dinosaur steeplechase race
- [ ] A dinosaur polo match
- [ ] Four sets of dinosaur cheerleaders
- [ ] Dinosaurs keeping score with their tails
- [ ] Some showjumping dinosaurs

PICTURE THIS

- [ ] A bird escaped from its frame
- [ ] An angry dragon
- [ ] An aeroplane with real wings
- [ ] An alarm clock
- [ ] A running cactus
- [ ] A cheeky tree trunk
- [ ] Some fish fingers
- [ ] A mermaid in reverse
- [ ] Three skiers
- [ ] A messy eater
- [ ] An upside-down picture
- [ ] A giant foot
- [ ] Three romantic animals
- [ ] A foot being tickled
- [ ] A picture within a picture
- [ ] Two men sharing the same hat
- [ ] Two helmets worn back-to-front
- [ ] Someone drinking through a straw
- [ ] Three flags
- [ ] Nine tongues hanging out
- [ ] A caveman escaped from his frame
- [ ] Seven dogs and a dogfish
- [ ] A bandaged finger
- [ ] A plaited moustache
- [ ] Four bears
- [ ] Three helmets with red plumes
- [ ] Four cats
- [ ] Four ducks
- [ ] Yellow, blue and red picture frames

THE GREAT RETREAT

- [ ] A shield suddenly vacated
- [ ] A heart on a soldier's tunic
- [ ] One curved sword
- [ ] A soldier carrying a hammer
- [ ] One striped spear
- [ ] A soldier not wearing a top
- [ ] Two run-away boots
- [ ] A horseless rider
- [ ] A soldier with a sword and an axe
- [ ] Three bare feet
- [ ] Four pink tails
- [ ] A spear with tips at both ends
- [ ] A helmet with a blue plume
- [ ] A soldier with a red boot and a blue boot
- [ ] A helmet with a red plume

WHAT A DOG FIGHT

- [ ] A gun dog soldier
- [ ] A guard dog soldier
- [ ] A boxer dog soldier
- [ ] A bloodhound soldier
- [ ] A Great Dane soldier
- [ ] A prize poodle soldier
- [ ] Two soldiers begging for bones
- [ ] Two soldiers running to fetch a ball
- [ ] Four stars on one tunic
- [ ] A dog basket
- [ ] A dog wearing a man mask
- [ ] Two fellow soldiers fighting each other
- [ ] Four ticklish feet
- [ ] A howling dog soldier
- [ ] A soldier with two tails
- [ ] A white star on a cream tunic
- [ ] Cream eyes on a white dog mask
- [ ] A soldier with black and brown legs
- [ ] A soldier with a black arm and a cream arm
- [ ] A cream glove on a blue striped arm
- [ ] A cream glove on a black striped arm
- [ ] A brown dog mask on a blue tunic
- [ ] A blue nose on a brown dog mask

THE BEAT OF THE DRUMS

- [ ] A cheeky back row
- [ ] Courtesy causing a pile-up
- [ ] Some very short spears
- [ ] A group facing in all directions
- [ ] A collision about to happen
- [ ] A knock-on effect
- [ ] Spears held upside down
- [ ] A never-ending spear
- [ ] Two hats joined together
- [ ] Some very scruffy soldiers
- [ ] A soldier wearing only one shoe
- [ ] A soldier wearing red shoes
- [ ] Thirty-five horses
- [ ] A pink hatband and a blue hatband
- [ ] One blue spear
- [ ] One lost shoe
- [ ] One hat with a yellow feather
- [ ] One hat with a red hatband

THE GREAT ESCAPE

- [ ] Ten men wearing green hoods
- [ ] Ten men wearing only one glove
- [ ] Ten men wearing hoods not matching gloves
- [ ] Ten men wearing two different coloured gloves
- [ ] Ten men wearing short and long gloves
- [ ] Ten lost gloves
- [ ] Ten men wearing one fingerless glove
- [ ] Six ladders
- [ ] Nineteen shovels
- [ ] Five question mark shapes formed by the hedge

HI WALLY-WATCHERS!

ARE YOU READY TO JOIN ME ON ANOTHER
INCREDIBLE ADVENTURE WITH MORE FUN
AND GAMES THAN EVER BEFORE?
I SEE SO MANY WONDERFUL THINGS ON MY
TRAVELS THAT THIS TIME I AM TAKING
MY NOTEPAD TO HELP ME REMEMBER THEM.
WOW! THE EXCITEMENT BEGINS RIGHT HERE
– AS THE RED KNIGHTS STORM THE BLUE
KNIGHTS' CASTLE WALLS. CAN YOU SPOT
SOME GRINNING GARGOYLES, A GHASTLY
GHOUL AND A GIANT CAKE?

THE SEARCH IS ON!

Wally

FIND WALLY, WOOF (BUT ALL YOU CAN SEE IS HIS TAIL), WENDA,
WIZARD WHITEBEARD AND ODLAW IN EVERY SCENE. (DON'T BE
FOOLED BY ANY CHILDREN THAT ARE DRESSED LIKE WALLY!)

FIND THE PRECIOUS THINGS THEY'VE LOST TOO:
WALLY'S KEY, WOOF'S BONE, WENDA'S CAMERA, WIZARD
WHITEBEARD'S SCROLL AND ODLAW'S BINOCULARS.

ONE MORE THING! CAN YOU FIND A PIECE OF PAPER THAT
WALLY HAS DROPPED FROM HIS NOTEPAD IN EVERY SCENE?

THE JURASSIC GAMES

GOODNESS CRETACEOUS! WHO WILL YOU SUPPORT FROM THE SIDELINES – THE BLUE STRIPY-SAURUS TEAM OR THE PINK SPOTTY-DOCUS TEAM? WILL YOU CHEER FOR THE CRICKET, THE ROWING OR THE BASKETBALL? DON'T FORGET TO WAVE IF YOU SEE A TREX – THEY'RE NOT IN ANY TEAM, BUT YOU WOULDN'T WANT TO GET ON THEIR WRONG SIDE!

PICTURE THIS

PHEW! LOOK AT ALL THESE FRAMED PORTRAITS. ALTHOUGH THEY MAY BE COLOURED DIFFERENTLY, SOME OF THESE ARE CHARACTERS I HAVE MET ON MY OTHER TRAVELS. THERE ARE ALSO SOME WHO APPEAR ELSEWHERE IN THIS BOOK. CAN YOU SPOT FOUR CHARACTERS THAT APPEAR TWICE IN THIS SPECTACULAR DISPLAY?

THE GREAT RETREAT

YIKES! A FEROCIOUS MAN-EATING
MONSTER IS WANDERING FREE
AND HE'S HUNGRY – HE'S GOBBLED
14 SOLDIERS FOR LUNCH ALREADY!
I'VE DRAWN THE SHAPES OF EIGHT
SOLDIERS ON THE RUN – CAN YOU
MATCH THEM WITH EIGHT SOLDIERS
IN THE CROWD BEFORE THE
MONSTER EATS THEM FOR HIS TEA?

WHAT A DOG FIGHT!

BOW WOW WOW! TWO ARMIES ARE LOCKED IN BATTLE, ALL WITH DOG MASKS ON. ONE ARMY IS DRESSED IN BLUE, BLACK AND WHITE, AND THE OTHER IN RED, BROWN AND CREAM. CAN YOU FIND EIGHT SOLDIERS, FOUR FROM EACH SIDE, WITH SOMETHING IN ONE OF THE OTHER SIDE'S COLOURS? OH, AND WHERE IS WOOF IN THIS DOGGY SCRUM?

THE BEAT OF THE DRUMS

BOOM BOOM BADOOM! WHAT AN ORDERLY SCENE! TWO ARMIES ARE STANDING TO ATTENTION SMARTLY DRESSED IN PINK AND BLUE. BUT SOME SOLDIERS ARE LETTING THE SIDE DOWN! CAN YOU FIND THE SOLDIER WHO HAS FORGOTTEN HIS SOCKS AND BOOTS AND 16 SOLDIERS STICKING OUT THEIR TONGUES?

THE GREAT ESCAPE

PHEW, WALLY-FOLLOWERS, I'M
HERE IN THIS A-MAZE-ING MAZE
AND I'M NOT THE ONLY ONE! FOUR
HOODED TEAMS ARE LOST IN HERE
AND CAN'T FIND A WAY OUT! SOME
HAVE INVENTED GREAT ESCAPES
– BY ROCKET, BY BALLOON AND BY
CATAPULT! THERE IS ONLY ONE WAY
THROUGH THIS MAZE – CAN YOU
HELP THEM FIND IT?

THE ENORMOUS PARTY

WOW! WHAT A BUZZ! ARE YOU
IN THE MOOD FOR A PARTY,
WALLY-WATCHERS? LOOK AT THE
BALLOONS, THE STREAMERS AND
ALL THE SMILING FACES! THE
FLAGS OF 18 COUNTRIES ARE
FLYING HERE – CAN YOU SPOT
SIX FLAGS THAT HAVE SOMETHING
WRONG WITH THEM? *

* THE ANSWERS ARE
IN PART TWO OF THE
CHECKLIST. NO
CHEATING!

THE GREAT WHERE'S WALLY?
THE INCREDIBLE PAPER CHASE CHECKLIST: PART TWO

THE ENORMOUS PARTY – ANSWERS

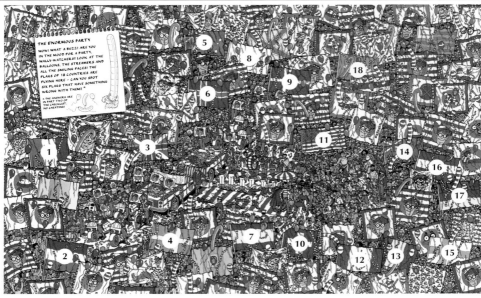

1 France
2 The Netherlands
3 United Kingdom
4 Sweden
5 Australia
6 Norway
7 Spain
8 Japan
9 Denmark

10 Switzerland
11 U.S.A.
12 Canada
13 Belgium
14 New Zealand
15 Finland
16 Austria
17 Federal Republic of Germany
18 Brazil

FLAGS WITH FAULTS
3 Diagonal red stripes missing
4 Flying the wrong way round
5 One star missing
11 Red and white stripes reversed
12 Maple leaf upside down
14 Diagonal red stripes missing

THE ENORMOUS PARTY

- Five back views of Wally's head
- A servant bending over backwards
- Two muscle-men being ignored
- An eight-man band
- A helmet worn back to front
- Eight front wheels
- Two upside-down faces of Wally
- A man wrapped in a streamer
- Someone wearing a blue beret
- A reluctant arm-rest

PENCIL AND PAPER

Did you find the eight tiny pieces of paper that Wally dropped from his notepad – one in every scene? Wally has left his pencil somewhere on the journey – can you go back and find it super-seekers?

AND TWO MORE THINGS!

Dozens of Wally-watchers appear in this book (there is at least one in every scene but some scenes have many more!).

There's another character – apart from Wally, Woof, Wenda, Wizard Whitebeard and Odlaw – in every scene. Can you find her?

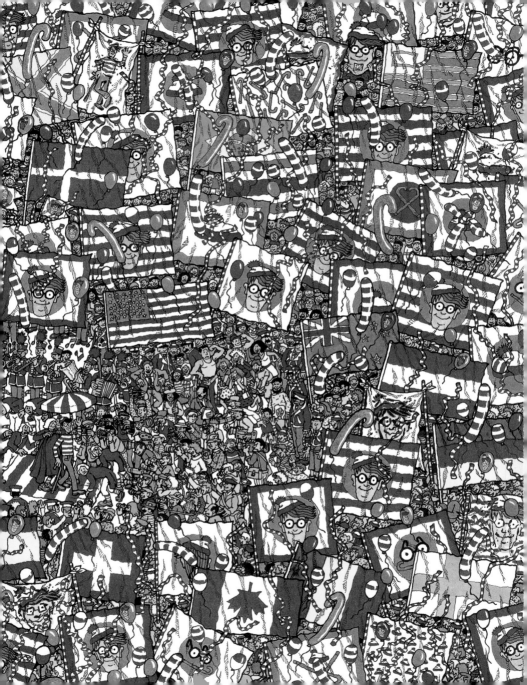

This edition published 2017 by Walker Books Ltd
87 Vauxhall Walk, London SE11 5HJ

6 8 10 9 7

This book has been typeset in Optima and Wallyfont.

Printed in China

British Library Cataloguing in Publication Data:
a catalogue record for this book is available from the British Library

ISBN 978-1-4063-7571-8

www.walker.co.uk